Riding Pillion with George Clooney

And Other Stories

Geraldine Ryan

Wrate's Publishing

First published in 2022 by Wrate's Publishing

ISBN 978-1-8383400-8-7

Copyright © 2022 by Geraldine Ryan

Edited and typeset by Wrate's Editing Services

www.wrateseditingservices.co.uk

Cover illustration and design: Rachel Middleton

A CIP catalogue record for this book is available from the British Library.

To my reader
The stories in this anthology have been written over a period of twenty years or so. I hope they will touch your heart; maybe one or two will even make you smile.

Contents

Riding Pillion with George Clooney

Bernadette tried not to mind that she was one of the few people on the tour travelling alone. Once off the plane and at baggage reclaim, she put on her shades and adopted the desultory pose of the frequent traveller, hoping to give off an air of mystery rather than one of desperation. As the luggage began to come out, her fellow passengers – with whom she'd travelled all the way from Dublin here to Bergamo Airport in Milan – suddenly roused themselves. They pushed forward, eagle-eyed and poised to pounce. One woman hurled herself with such force onto her luggage when it finally arrived, you'd have thought she'd been reunited with a long-lost relative. Deciding she was having nothing to do with this unseemly behaviour, Bernadette turned away and tried to distract herself by attempting to read the adverts on the surrounding walls. It occurred to her she should have brought a phrase book. Mammy – if she were alive and here with her now – would have been right there in the middle of that scrum and Da would no doubt be shouting orders from the back. Neither of them cared a jot about what other people thought of them. Whereas, sometimes, Bernadette wondered if this was all she cared about.

What did people imagine her to be when they looked at her, she wondered? *If* they ever looked at her. Hopefully, not plain old Bernadette McNaboe from Ballyclonhead, who worked for the council and still lived with her widowed father even though she'd just turned fifty.

A recently widowed mafia wife, perhaps, fleeing north to Milan to escape her husband's enemies who suspected she knew too much? Or a fading film actress, travelling incognito to avoid the paparazzi, on her way to meet her married lover for a secret rendezvous?

Casually turning over these two alternatives in her mind, it occurred to her how all the interesting words – the ones that spelled intrigue and passion – seemed to be foreign ones. Funny, that!

By the time her case showed up, everyone had disappeared. When she located the rest of her group by the exit, she sensed a crackle of irritation running through it. She even thought she heard a woman mutter to her husband that she could have sworn she'd seen that bright blue suitcase go round three times, so how on earth the owner could have missed it and kept them all waiting she had no idea.

It wasn't a very good start, was it, getting everybody's backs up by arriving late at the meeting point? And she with impeccable time keeping as a rule, too! Bernadette, blushing furiously, muttered an awkward apology as she dragged her case over to the driver, who stashed it in the hold with the others. His welcoming smile and cheery 'Bongiorno' went some way to softening the bruising glares of some of her fellow passengers as she took her seat on the coach. As did the effusive reassurance from Karen, who introduced herself as their guide for the next seven days. Bernadette was not to worry that she'd kept them waiting, Karen insisted. It had given everyone else time to get to know each other.

Lovely she was, Bernadette decided. Her own age, probably, but slim and elegant and effortlessly stylish, with a lovely tan, gorgeous hair and milky white, even teeth in a beautiful smile.

As they joined the motorway, Bernadette found herself only half listening to Karen's running commentary. She was much more interested in observing her fellow travellers. Her earlier suspicions at the airport seemed to be confirmed. She was definitely the only person travelling alone. The youngest, too, by some ten years if she were any judge of age.

Already, the fizzy bubbles of anticipation she'd

experienced on and off ever since booking this autumn holiday back in March were beginning to go flat. Had she made a mistake booking with this tour group? Should she have gone for something more adventurous that would have attracted a younger crowd?

But then, where would she have fitted in on an adventure holiday? The most adventurous physical challenge she'd ever attempted was getting in the back of Mickey Rourke's boneshaker.

She told herself to snap out of it before it got worse. It's not like she'd come to Italy with the sole purpose of having a holiday romance. Not at all! She'd come for the scenery. The lakes – Como, Maggiore, Lugano, and for the two-hour rail climb up the Alps as far as St Moritz, the playground of the rich and famous.

But she'd have been lying to herself if – in her idle moments – she hadn't considered the possibility of meeting a like-minded soul of the opposite sex on her trip. Fat chance with any of the men here, though. Even if you discounted the fact they all looked terribly married, a good half of them must have been the same age as her father.

The thought of Da set her off worrying about him. He'd grown even grumpier than usual as the date of her trip approached. All last week there'd been little jibes at her 'going off gallivanting'. Complaints, too, about the latest ache in his joints and a worry that his sciatica might be coming back. She knew all about aches and pains. Her father was one big pain in the backside. Couldn't he be gracious and allow her one week out of fifty-two to spend as she wanted?

It's not as if he was fit enough to go with her on this trip anyway. It was a well-known fact he got stiff if he sat too long, and there'd be long stretches of time spent in the coach, she reminded him. Not to mention all that foreign food. If he were deprived of his rashers and potatoes for more than two days running you wouldn't hear the end of it.

Knowing she was right about how little this type of holiday would suit him did little to make him more conciliatory towards her, though. Take the last dig he'd fired off at her at six o'clock this morning, just as she was leaving.

At the time, she'd been hauling her case into the back of Mickey's old banger. Her father had come hobbling out with her passport and her boarding ticket, which – much to her embarrassment – she'd left on the kitchen dresser.

'How you'll find your way around a foreign country, even with a guide to look after you, I'll never know,' he'd remarked, handing it over to her while sending Mickey a man-to-man look which said simply, 'Women. What are they like!'

She'd been too busy covering up her mortification to snap back. Too busy, too, offering up prayers to every saint she knew for Mickey's van to get them all the way to the airport without breaking down.

Had it been up to her, and even though it would have cost the earth, she'd have booked a taxi, but Mickey had been so insistent, coming round to the house, nervously clutching his cap in both hands, and offering not only to drive her to the airport but to pick her up on her return. Practically press-ganged into it, she'd been. She'd insisted on paying for the petrol, of course. She didn't want to be beholden to him.

To his credit, Mickey hadn't responded to her father's coded message. He'd just straightened his cap and opened the passenger door. She'd climbed in, pulling her skirt down over her knees and wishing she'd worn trousers, remembering Mickey's habit of looking at her legs while pretending not to.

Perhaps it was just as well she couldn't think of a clever come back, she thought now, turning her head to look at the changing scenery through the window. She didn't want to leave home on a sour note, especially not with a plane journey ahead of her and no knowing whether she'd land safely at the other end. Planes were dropping out of the sky like dead birds these days.

She'd give Da a ring as soon as she got to her hotel. Make sure he was all right. Perhaps she should call Mickey, too. Make sure he'd got back to Ballyclonhead in one piece.

* * *

Karen had been a tour guide with Far and Wide Holidays for more years than she cared to remember. She didn't like to boast, but she was confident she'd become an expert on the clientele Far and Wide typically attracted. They were mostly couples, with no one younger than 55 – many more were much older. Not wealthy, by any means, but comfortable enough to be able to afford at least a couple of holidays a year if they budgeted.

On the whole, she'd always found them to be an agreeable lot. You got your complainers, of course – she'd already earmarked the rather large woman with the big hair and the small husband as this group's chief moaner, and she had her charm offensive planned to the last detail. She'd *make* the woman like her *and* enjoy the tour, too, whatever it took! She'd never had an unhappy client, and she wasn't about to start getting one now, on this the final tour of the season.

In every group, there was always a straggler or two. Was the middle-aged lady with the brown clothes and the blue suitcase this week's straggler, she wondered, or was this the first and only time she'd be bringing up the rear? Poor thing. She couldn't help feeling sorry for her. It was obvious she'd overheard the complaining woman's loudly whispered remark and was still smarting from it.

Thank God for Paulo and his sunny nature. His smile had gone a long way to de-flustering the poor lady. Karen decided to make a special effort with her. She would send her home with some memories to treasure if it were the last thing she did.

* * *

Once Bernadette had finished her little tour of her allocated room, she plonked herself down on her single bed and thought about it all. She'd noticed there were plenty of hangers in the wardrobe after all, so she was a bit annoyed with herself for listening to Mary Stone's exhortations to pack more because hotels never provided enough.

If only she'd listened to Mary's other bit of advice about taking a travel kettle, a few teabags and some of those little pots of long-life milk. Having searched high and low, she'd discovered Mary was dead on with her remark about the lack of tea-making facilities in hotels on the continent. Now she'd have to drink tap water from the bathroom. Was that even safe?

She was a bit worried about the shower, too, because it looked very different from the one at home. Dad's words of this morning came back to her. *How you'll find your way around a foreign country, even with a guide to look after you, I'll never know.*

Oh, he'd be loving this right now. Her sitting here

out of her depth, worrying about how to work the damn shower. If he were here to listen to her concerns – that she'd never get friendly with anyone on this trip because already she'd got herself a reputation as a troublemaker – he would agree wholeheartedly. No doubt he'd tell her to hop on the next plane and come home where she belonged.

Well, he wasn't here, was he? She should listen to that small voice of reason whispering in her ear. Bernadette got up from her bed and went over to the French window. It led onto a window ledge that only someone with the wildest of imaginations could say was a balcony. But what of it? It was as near to a balcony as mattered. As soon as she got hold of a postcard she'd write to Da and tell him that she had one.

She definitely had a view. And surely a view more than made up for a shower she couldn't work, a suitcase half-full of unnecessary coat hangers and the lack of tea-making facilities?

It would be dark in an hour or so, but even now, all the little lights in the cluster of villas that hugged the bay were coming on, one after the other, twinkling like fairy lights on a Christmas tree. She opened her window and listened to the sounds of the street drift upwards.

Passing cars, of course – you couldn't go anywhere these days without the roar of traffic in your ear. The occasional slap and clap of lake water against a moored motorboat. People calling out to one another in Italian, the smell of their cigarette smoke mingling with the delicious aroma of the food from the hotel kitchen. Oh, it was all so magical.

A glance at her watch told her it would be six o'clock in Ireland. Da would be at the table now, tucking into the stew she'd made him last night between bouts of packing and reminding him to take his medication and put the right bin out on the right morning for the binmen.

Best to leave it awhile. He was bound to have some complaint that would spoil her magical mood. And like all Da's complaints, they'd still be there in the morning. Doubtless with the addition of one or two new ones.

She also had second thoughts about ringing Mickey. Wouldn't it look a bit odd, her ringing him up to enquire after his safety when *she* was the one who'd been on a plane?

Besides, she didn't want to give him the wrong idea. She'd known Mickey Rourke ever since she could remember – they'd gone through school together. At one time, they'd even been out on a couple of dates. It was when Mammy first got ill, and she'd been worried to death about the prognosis.

Mickey had proved a good friend, appearing not to mind her remoteness. In the pub, after they'd come out of the cinema, he'd chattered away about the film they'd just seen while she'd just sat there silently, staring into space and brooding.

When things got worse with Mammy, she told him she no longer had the time or the energy to go out to the cinema or the pub with him. He'd taken it well and stepped away.

Ever since then, he'd maintained a respectful distance, for which she told herself she was grateful. Perhaps, in the circumstances, it might be best if she restricted herself to a postcard, reminding him what time she'd be landing once the holiday was over. She didn't want to give him false hopes, she thought, picking up her wash bag.

Not a one-off, then. The straggler arrived in the dining room just as Karen was leaving, thoughts of what she had to do before tomorrow's excursion buzzing in her head. It had been a long season, starting way back in March, and she was tired. It was easy to slip up when tired, and she didn't want to risk disappointing her final group of the season.

It might be her seventh trip to this hotel, and she might be heartily sick of the menu, which she knew like the back of her hand, but to the group who'd arrived this evening for their week's holiday, all this was a new experience.

She'd hoped to slide past after her cheery 'buon

appetito' and disappear into her room. But the woman – what was her name again? – something very Irish, a saint's name – Brigitte – no, Bernadette, that was it – well, she looked so overwhelmed and so forlorn standing there alone, holding open the door for Karen to pass through, that she knew she'd have it on her conscience all evening if she didn't try and straighten the poor woman out.

'Oh, I didn't mean to be late,' Bernadette said, her voice tremulous, as if she were on the verge of tears. 'Only . . .'

There followed a long and convoluted tale about her trying to get the shower to work. As far as Karen could make out, the gist of it was that she'd been a bit enthusiastic turning on the tap and water had gone all over the floor. She'd had to mop it up with the towels, which had not only made her late for dinner but had left her with nothing to dry herself with in the morning.

'Well, we'll soon fix that,' Karen reassured her. 'I'll pop to reception on my way back to my room and get someone to take some fresh towels up to yours right away. Room two hundred and seventeen, isn't it?'

Bernadette nodded gratefully and smiled a tremulous little smile.

'Now, we need to get you a table.'

Karen deftly steered her in the direction of a table for six occupied by only five people. She offered up a fervent prayer that they weren't expecting a sixth member of their party. She strongly suspected Bernadette would take this as a personal rejection and be mortified. Thankfully, her prayers were answered. Somebody's husband was too exhausted to eat after the journey and had gone straight to bed. Gratefully, Bernadette took the husband's place, thanking the woman who'd given this information profusely and offering her sympathies to the indisposed spouse. As soon as she could be certain that the two were hitting it off, Karen took her leave with a cheery wave. It seemed that for tonight, at least, her work was done.

It was nice of Karen to find her a seat at Grace's table. The poor woman's husband had been unable to face eating his dinner in public. Apparently, he'd taken one look at the vast dining room packed to the roof and buzzing with chatter and had turned on his heels.

Bernadette didn't blame him. She would have liked to do the same thing herself. She must have read something on the company website about the size of the dining room before booking the holiday, but she couldn't remember. Honestly, though, if you had to get up at some point to pay a visit to the ladies', you'd need a map to find yourself back to your table.

'Would you like a bread roll?'

Her new friend's question startled Bernadette. She

took one from the proffered basket with rather more enthusiasm than a bread roll could possibly merit.

'That's very kind of you,' she said. 'I'm Bernadette by the way. What's your name?'

* * *

'Did you know George Clooney has a villa along this stretch?

It was Day Five, and they were off to Switzerland, which was where Lake Lugano was just about situated. Bernadette *didn't* know this. Actually, at seven thirty in the morning, battling her way round the dining room, already late for the eight o'clock start, she felt she knew very little about anything.

It was Grace who was addressing her. Grace with the husband who hadn't turned up to dinner that first night. She had a bowl of cereal in one hand and a cup of coffee in the other. When she put the cup down, Bernadette felt her heart sink. It meant Grace was here for the long haul.

She was very nice, was Grace, and so was her husband. Everyone was nice, no doubt about it. Even the woman with the big hair and the small husband appeared to have got over being kept waiting at the airport that first day. It was just . . .

Well, for a start, Bernadette liked a quiet breakfast. She was no great talker at the best of times – had always preferred listening to speaking. That was one thing she'd say in Mickey Rourke's favour. The way he didn't feel obliged to fill a silence all the time.

She'd particularly appreciated that on their recent drive to the airport. It was like he'd sensed she was stressed, what with worrying about the flight and about Da. He must have guessed that she'd be going over in her head everything she'd packed in case there was something she'd forgotten and would need to go back for before they got too far.

'I didn't know that, no,' she said, politely.

'We saw it from the slow ferry yesterday on our day off. You'd have seen it, too, if you'd come with us.'

Was she being chided, Bernadette wondered? She'd stayed behind yesterday when Grace and her husband, along with Rona and Joe, another couple who appeared to have taken Bernadette under their wing, took the opportunity of their one excursion-free day to do a bit of exploring themselves.

The truth was, she was exhausted. The lakes were lovely, but it seemed to her that everywhere they went entailed a three-hour return trip in the coach round winding roads. Pleading a headache, she'd stayed in her room and read her book. Apart from her conscience, which refused to leave her alone, it had been bliss. She'd known it was the perfect time to ring Da for a good, long chat, and the thought kept on nagging. I'll do it when I get to the end of this chapter, she kept saying to herself. But in the end, she never did ring him. He'd have wanted to know why she wasn't out with the rest of them, and if she'd said why she knew he wouldn't be able to resist replying, 'I told you so.'

Her conscience had got the better of her in the end, though, as she'd guessed it would. She'd stepped outside in the afternoon and bought a postcard, hastily scribbling a few words on the back of it. Actually, she'd bought two postcards. The second one was for Mickey. It took her ages to think up something interesting to write; something a bit less obvious than, 'Wish you were here.'

She handed over Dad's at the reception desk, to be franked and posted. But in the end, she held onto Mickey's. Reading back through what she'd written, she decided it would be highly inappropriate to send it. He was bound to get the wrong idea.

Karen waited till she saw Bernadette peel away from Grace and make her way towards a table with her cup of coffee and croissant. Then she went over to speak to her. Bernadette looked startled as she noticed her approach.

'I won't be a minute, honestly,' Bernadette said, clumsily smearing jam on her pastry.

'No, please. Don't worry. You still have twenty minutes before the coach leaves."

'Ah, yes. Switzerland,' Bernadette said.

It would be cold up there in the Alps, so she needed to make sure she dressed for it.

'I only popped over to say you don't need to worry about the postcard.'

Bernadette gave her a look of total incomprehension.

'Leastways, I saw your signature on the bottom and put two and two together. I guess you must have accidentally dropped it, and someone picked it up. I found it on a table in the lounge, so I took it over to reception and asked them to post it.'

Bernadette, her croissant halfway to her mouth, seemed to freeze

'You posted my card?' she gasped.

Karen knew at once she'd done the wrong thing. Should she insist she hadn't read it? Or would Bernadette know that she was lying? It had been impossible not to, of course.

'Dear Mickey', it had said. 'I think you'd love Lake Como. It is very still and deep, a bit like you. I think you'd like a different sort of hotel, though, because sometimes you can't hear yourself think when you're eating your food. Bernadette. I miss you.' There were three kisses.

'I'm sorry,' Karen said. 'I should have returned it to you. I just thought . . .'

What had she just thought? That she knew how

people should run their lives better than they did themselves? She'd been in this job too long!

'No, no,' Bernadette mumbled. 'I thought I'd put it in my bag. Obviously, I hadn't.'

She turned her gaze back to her croissant.

Karen was beginning to wish the earth would swallow her up. 'So, fifteen minutes, then?' she said, affecting a breezy tone.

'Yes. Fifteen minutes,' Bernadette echoed.

Karen, desperate to be somewhere else, smiled awkwardly and turned away. Halfway to the exit, she looked back over her shoulder. Bernadette was still sitting there, staring into space. She hoped she would get to the coach on time. The Bernina Express would wait for no one.

She'd never be able to look the woman in the eye again. Thank God they'd be going home in two days, and she wouldn't have to see Karen again. What must she think of her, a woman her age acting like a lovesick girl?

She didn't know why she'd picked up that second card in the gift shop yesterday and taken it to the man at the counter. One card seemed so pathetic somehow. It marked her out as a woman with no friends. There she was again, concerning herself with what complete strangers thought of her.

Once, she'd made the mistake of telling Mickey this. God knows why she'd confided something so intimate. Maybe it was because she knew he wouldn't judge her for it. He seemed to like her as she was, which was something she found hard to understand. Who was she, after all? Just plain old invisible Bernadette McNaboe.

Bernadette, with twenty seconds to spare, took the last empty seat on the coach. Immediately, they were off. She only caught the tail end of what Karen was saying. Something about it being early and how – though the lake was covered in mist still and it would be a few hours before the sun was out – they'd be sure to see it on the way back. Grace, apparently, was absolutely correct, she continued. George Clooney *did* have a villa on Lake Como. And here it was on the left, by the little church and the single cypress tree. Everyone, including Bernadette, turned their heads to stare, but they couldn't see a thing.

Bernadette closed her eyes and rested her head on the back of the seat. Karen knew a lot about George Clooney and how he spent his time at Villa Oleandra, just as she knew a lot about everything else that went on in this part of Italy, past and present.

She told them that George had been here in the summer, with his wife and Robert de Niro, and Robert de Niro's wife. And that he loved the place. But there were rumours he might sell it because he could no longer get the privacy he craved.

The last thing she heard before slipping into sleep was something about George owning a Harley Davison, and how he liked to tear around the island on it. She found herself dreaming. She was sitting on the pillion seat of George's bike, her arms around him. They were going very fast, and it was thrilling. Each time they came to a bend, she leaned into it, clinging even tighter to George.

But when he turned round to smile at her, it wasn't George at all. It was Mickey Rourke! Bernadette shook herself awake. She must have squealed in her sleep because the woman sitting across the aisle was staring at her, like she was some sort of loon.

'You woke up just in time,' she said. 'Here we are at the train station.'

Climbing up to the Alps on the lovely little train, Bernadette had been able to forget that before she got home, Mickey Rourke would receive a postcard from her telling him she thought he was as deep as Lake Como, and that she missed him. She even managed to forget that most disturbing dream.

But once back in her hotel room, and for the last two days of her holiday, it was all she could think about. Was it too late to ring Da and get him to tell Mickey she didn't need a lift from the airport after all?

The trouble was, she did need it. She'd left it far too late to prebook a cab.

She was a bag of nerves on the plane. This time, at baggage reclaim, she didn't take her eyes off the conveyor belt for a second. She just wanted to get her bag and get out of there. She would just have to face the music. There was no point denying to Mickey that she'd sent that card. What on earth would she say when she saw him?

He was there, at the gate, grinning. He wasn't wearing his cap today, and she noticed his curls for the first time. He'd made an effort with the rest of him, too, and was wearing a nice blue shirt and a blue tie that matched his eyes. He was holding a card in his hands with her name written on it, like he was a professional driver, and she was a businesswoman being met at the airport by her chauffeur.

She couldn't help smiling back at him when she saw his little joke, and her reaction made his grin even wider. She walked towards him, afraid to look him in the eye.

'Welcome home,' he said, taking her bag, even though she made a fuss and said she could carry it herself.

They walked in silence to the van. Mickey stashed her case in the boot and opened the door for her. There was a bunch of flowers on her seat. Flowers. He'd bought her flowers.

'I got your card,' he said.

'Oh.'

'I wondered,' he began, hesitantly. 'If, maybe, we could stop halfway. There's a nice little pub – well, it looks nice from the outside. I'd only have an orange juice, of course, what with me driving and that.'

She'd never known him say so much in one breath. He was as nervous as she was. One of them was going to have to calm down. It might as well be her.

'That sounds like a grand idea, Mickey,' she said, raising the bunch of flowers to her nose and sniffing them in appreciation.

'They're from the garage,' he said. 'Modern flowers don't smell of anything anymore.'

'Maybe not,' she said. 'But they look lovely.'

She was glad to be back. She'd enjoyed her holiday – to a certain extent. In a short while, she'd be back home with Da, listening to him grumble about his week. But the prospect didn't make her heart sink anymore. Not now.

'Mickey,' she said, turning to him at last and holding his blue-eyed gaze. 'Have you ever thought about getting a motorbike?'

He chuckled. 'What man hasn't?' he said. 'Why, do you fancy riding pillion?'

Right now, riding pillion with Mickey Rourke sounded a grand idea

'I do,' she said.

So that was it. The end of the season. The hotel would be closing till March and Como would be empty apart from a few souls. She hoped they'd had a good time, her final group of the year. She hoped they thought she'd been a good tour manager.

From the size of the tip she'd given her, the complaining woman seemed to be satisfied. And she'd had generous tips, hugs and good reviews from everyone else, too.

Bernadette, though. That business with the postcard continued to play on her mind. The poor woman had been so anxious when she boarded the coach for the last time for the return trip to the airport. You'd have thought she was going home to her death. She'd promised herself at the start of the tour that she'd send Bernadette home with some special memories. How had she managed to fail so badly?

The more she thought about it, the more she wondered if she was losing her touch. Perhaps it really was time to start thinking seriously about packing the job in. She'd be fifty-two next month. How much longer could she keep up this pace – the travelling, the hotels, and the stress of being responsible for other people all the time?

Maybe she should give her old friend Jo a call. Last time they'd met up, Jo had made her an offer to join her business. Made In Heaven, it was called. A dating bureau for the over-fifties. It would be a change from what she was doing now, that was for sure.

But then she thought about Bernadette and the mess she'd made by posting that card to the man named Mickey. No, maybe she should stick this job out, for another season at least. Because, really, what did she know about matchmaking?

First published 2010, *Woman's Weekly*

A Butterfly Stirring

Millie poured milk onto her cornflakes, basking in the reflection that today was the first day of the summer holidays. The next six weeks stretched ahead, full of glorious promise.

'Poor Gran shouldn't be on her own after an operation.'

Mum's words broke into her contented silence. She wished Mum would hurry up and find her car keys. She wasn't usually so flustered in the morning.

'It's only a minor op, I thought,' Millie said.

'Yes, but even so. Ah! Here they are! Exactly where I left them in the first place!'

Finally, thought Millie. Except she'd put them down again.

'Anyway, I've been thinking about it,' Mum said.

'About what?'

'About Gran. And I've come up with a solution.'

Millie put down her spoon. Her mother was a human resources manager. People were her business, she often said. She had a flair for getting them to do exactly what she wanted, which is why Millie was beginning to get more than a little suspicious.

'You'd be a wonderful tonic for Gran, you know you would. Such a help after her operation.'

And there it was. Millie willed her mother's words to go away.

'That poster on your wall, Millie – the one with the butterfly. Remind me what it says again.'

'A butterfly stirring the air today in Beijing can transform the storm systems next month in New York,' she sullenly replied, before lifting her spoon to her mouth.

'Well, here's your chance to make a small ripple!' Her mother was beaming encouragingly. 'You know how busy I am at work in the summer months, trying to cover all the staffing arrangements while people take their annual leave?'

Millie nodded into her cornflakes.

'Well,' her mother continued, 'because of your kind action in volunteering to look after Gran for a couple of weeks, she'll recover sooner, and I'll be able to do my job without worrying too much about her. Which will mean that I'll be more effective as a human resources manager, which in turn will mean that every member of personnel will—'

'Yeah, all right, Mum. I get the picture.' Millie sighed.

Her mother was good, she had to admit – very good. And so it was that two days later, having been deposited at Gran's, instead of doing nothing, Millie ended up doing her shopping.

Forlornly, she wheeled Gran's clapped-out old bike around the village, in the vain hope she might find some action. There was no one about, of course. No one interesting, at any rate, and definitely no good-looking boys. The average age of the population must be at least sixty-five, Millie soon decided. She also decided that applying lip gloss and mascara before setting out had been a complete waste of effort.

On the way back to Gran's, she popped into the newsagent's for a browse. She wondered if Gran's paperboy might be there. She'd caught a glimpse of him through her bedroom window that morning, having been motivated enough to get out of bed with the intention of scowling at whoever was responsible for the loud, tuneless whistle that had woken her up at such a godforsaken hour.

Of course, she'd only managed to glimpse his back view as he retreated down the path and mounted his bike. But that one peek had been promising – long legs and exactly the right amount of swagger. His face, as he swung himself athletically onto his saddle and swept off down the road, had been partly obscured by his baseball cap, but she'd noticed a good, firm jawline and no spots.

Inside the newsagent's, she flicked through the magazines, turning her head every time the door opened, just in case he made an appearance, but there was no sign of him. Then it occurred to her, not without a twinge of envy, that unlike her, he probably had friends.

No doubt they were all down at the swimming pool and not stuck like her with a gran whose own daughter placed her precious job first and left a mere child of fifteen to play the caring role in her place.

Millie wasn't uncaring by nature. She loved her gran a lot. Remembering her butterfly poster with a twinge of conscience, she promised to be extra nice to her once she got back, to make up for her bitter thoughts.

After a while, the lady behind the counter gave a cough and asked Millie was there anything she could help her with.

'If you're looking for a magazine that isn't out yet, we can always deliver it when it comes in,' she said, with a friendly smile.

This is meant to be, Millie decided, as she freewheeled back to Gran's. Once the paperboy – she briefly wondered what his name might be – knew there was a girl of about his own age staying with Mrs Conway, then he might well make the next move. If she wasn't mistaken, things were beginning to look up.

That afternoon, however, her mood took another dive, and she began to think that the day – and the visit – had gone on long enough. This paperboy surely had more exciting things to do than study the contents of his delivery bag. He'd probably just shove her *Mizz* through the door, alongside Gran's *Telegraph* and *Woman's Weekly*, without so much as a backward glance.

'I'm just going outside to do a bit of pottering,' Mrs Conway called out to Millie from the kitchen, as the afternoon sun began its retreat from her front garden.

By nature, Mrs Conway was an active woman who hated to be made a fuss of. Her granddaughter was a delight and would do anything for her, but she was young. She didn't see the weeds that were beginning to take hold in her flowerbeds, and she probably hadn't noticed that the grass needed cutting.

Briefly, Millie looked up from the TV screen. 'Positively no weeding now, Gran – you've got to promise me. I'll do some later, after *Neighbours*. You must show me how your lawnmower works.'

Mrs Conway felt a twinge of conscience. Millie never failed to surprise her. Like generations of teenage girls before her, she affected to be cool and bolshy, but inside she cared so much about other people's welfare and feelings.

'You're a sweet girl, Millie.' Mrs Conway had made her way back into the lounge by slow degrees. 'I doubt every girl your age would have given up two weeks of her precious summer holidays to act as housemaid to her crock of a grandmother.'

Millie hoped her blushes weren't too obvious. Had her mother really said she'd volunteered?

'Well, you know what I always say, Gran,' she said, putting on her sweetest smile. 'A butterfly stirring the air today in Beijing can transform the storm systems next month in New York.'

'What, dear?'

Mrs Conway, only half-listening, was rummaging around for her secateurs, which she could have sworn she'd last seen in this room.

'Oh, dear,' she muttered. 'Since I've come out of hospital my memory's melted into fudge.'

Putting her hands in her apron pocket, she realised they'd been there all along. Millie smiled at her indulgently.

Outside, the air was still warm, filled with the fragrance of roses. Mrs Conway bent low to snip a particularly enchanting bud and held it to her nostrils. Down here, away from the sight of the road, she could almost believe herself to be in the depths of the countryside.

She closed her eyes in appreciation. How wonderful it was to be back in her own garden and to smell the scents and hear the sounds of summer. How much more she was going to appreciate them this year, she resolved, after a week spent in hospital with nothing but antiseptic or unappetising dinners to smell and the sound of trolleys being wheeled around the wards or the complaints of her fellow patients to listen to.

Mrs Conway's peace was suddenly shattered. Someone was singing loudly and hopelessly off-key. There followed another layer of this ear-splitting cacophony, this time emitting from the lusty lungs of a baby, who took up the chorus in a series of airwave-shattering wails.

Mrs Conway's hands involuntarily flew up to her ears. She stood up just as the woman, the baby and the pram passed her hedge, and glared at all three.

'Oh, I didn't see you there!'

Jenna Murphy, startled by Mrs Conway's sudden appearance from behind her garden hedge, pulled up. She wondered whether all the people round here were so unfriendly. All she'd been trying to do was to cheer poor Charlie up. He'd been teething all day and crying for most of it. She'd been confident that she might just manage to coax a smile out of him with her all-singing, all-dancing performance down the street, but now this dragon had made everything worse, jumping out of nowhere like that.

Mrs Conway opened her mouth to speak. She'd intended making some remark that was cutting and to the point. Whose garden was it she was standing in, anyway? She didn't think she'd ever have to ask permission to stand in her own garden from some young flibbertigibbet with a pierced navel and a skirt that barely covered her bottom!

Just as she was gearing herself up and beginning to search through her memory bank of cutting lines, she saw the butterfly. It hovered on the almost audible silence that preceded the baby's next loud wail. It alighted on the handlebar of the pram, a myriad of iridescent colours, its perfect wings trembling with profound grace.

In the very moment Mrs Conway's gaze was drawn towards it, Jenna saw it, too. And so did Charlie, who swallowed his next wail even before it emerged from his mouth. In one brief, transforming moment, his face became a picture of joy. Spellbound, he pointed a chubby finger at the butterfly and beamed at the two women who looked on.

In that moment of magic, Mrs Conway remembered Millie's words: 'A butterfly stirring the air today in Beijing can transform the storm systems next month in New York.'

'I'm sorry if I startled you,' she said simply. 'I didn't mean to frighten your baby like that.'

Jenna bit her lip. Perhaps she'd got the old lady wrong. 'No, really,' she stammered. 'It's me who should be apologising. After all, I'm no Charlotte Church. Oh, and by the way,' she added, 'Charlie's not my baby. I'm only the nanny.'

Charlie clapped his hands again and followed the butterfly with his eyes as it lifted itself into the air and flew away.

'Beautiful creatures, aren't they?' Jenna said, then made a face at Charlie, who chuckled back in appreciation. 'I'm talking about butterflies, not babies,' she added, for the benefit of her new acquaintance.

'You don't mean that, really,' Mrs Conway said. 'You're a natural with babies, anyone can see that. I'm sure the baby's parents have every confidence in you.'

Jenna blushed. What a nice old lady this was, she decided. Suddenly shy, she said, 'Well, I'd better get this little chap home. Maybe I'll see you again soon.'

Mrs Conway nodded amiably. 'I promise not to jump out on you next time,' she said with a smile.

Tom Drake, Mrs Conway's new neighbour three doors down, was washing his car half-heartedly. What he'd rather be doing was sitting in the garden with a bottle of ice-cold lager and listening to the cricket scores on the radio. But then there was still all that unpacking to do. Not for the first time since contracts had been exchanged, he wondered if he'd made a mistake moving to this street. He'd been here a week now and not a soul had spoken to him yet.

He looked up as footsteps passed his house. A pretty, young woman was pushing a pram and babbling enthusiastically to a chuckling baby. She appeared to be tap dancing.

'Lovely day,' Jenna Murphy called out, slowing down. She'd got it wrong about the people who lived round here, she decided – all they needed was a bit of encouragement.

'Just moved in, have you?' she added. 'Charlie and I were watching the removal van, weren't we, Charlie? We live next door.'

Charlie grinned at Tom, who returned it.

'Say something quickly,' he urged himself, 'or else she'll disappear into the house next door and that will be that.'

Trust the most attractive woman he'd met in ages to be married and with a baby, too! He might have a nice car and be earning enough to buy his own property, but as far as women were concerned, he decided he was doomed.

'Your baby looks just like you,' he said, to keep her talking a bit longer.

Jenna grinned. 'Oh, Charlie's not mine. I'm only the hired hand,' she said. 'After six o'clock, I occupy a child-free zone.'

Tom gulped. Was she asking him out? He decided moving to this neighbourhood was the best decision he'd ever made.

An approaching tuneless whistle signalled the arrival of the paperboy on his evening round.

'This yours?' Darren Barton thrust a copy of *Mizz* magazine at Tom. It didn't look like the sort of thing a grown man would read, but he prided himself on minding his own business.

Tom Drake made a royal effort to refrain from asking if he looked like the kind of guy who read magazines intended for teenage girls, but he didn't want his new neighbour thinking he was a pompous ignoramus. He could see that being pompous would get him nowhere with a girl who wore a ring in her navel and who tap-danced down the street.

'What number does it say, mate?' Tom asked instead.

'Thirty-nine,' Darren replied, his brow furrowed. 'But that's old Mrs Conway's house. Unless . . .' Darren scratched his head through his baseball cap. Perhaps he hadn't imagined that girl glaring at him from an upstairs window this morning after all? He'd go and knock on the door now; it was the only way to find out. He half-hoped she'd come to the door and speak to him herself. It was only the third day of his holidays and already he was bored silly. Most of his mates had gone away – which was why he'd taken on an evening round in addition to his morning one, for something to do.

Mrs Conway heard the front doorbell ring and glanced through her bedroom window, but she didn't bother to answer it. It was only the paperboy. She'd let Millie get it.

The day was turning into a lovely evening. Perhaps she'd just close her eyes for five minutes. Voices drifted through her open window. She should have asked that nice young woman for her name. She seemed to be hitting it off with that new neighbour she'd not yet had the opportunity to introduce herself to.

She could hear Millie, too, suddenly animated, chattering nineteen to the dozen with the paperboy. Nice, polite boy, that Darren. Sleep overcame her suddenly; a sweet, healing and refreshing sleep. And with it, a dream of butterflies.

First published 2001, *Woman's Weekly*

Our Solemn Promise

Back when we were in Mrs Jenkins' class at primary school, my best friend Gemma and I promised each other we'd be bridesmaid at each other's wedding. All through secondary school, we continued to be the closest of friends and occasionally reminded each other of our old pledge.

We may have teased each other about the chances of the other ever managing to snare anyone long enough for him to want to walk up the aisle with her, but we always ended our conversation by swearing that if it did happen, and we did find someone we wanted to marry and who wanted to marry us too, then this was what we'd do.

Even when I moved away to London and she remained behind in the small town where we'd both grown up, we still messaged each other every day. We might not see each other for months at a time, but within minutes of us getting together again we'd take up exactly as we'd left off, and it would be as if no time had passed at all.

I'd made a lot of friends since, but no one had ever come close to replacing Gemma as my best friend. So, when Nick and I set a date, the first person I rang – even before my parents – was her. I told her the date and the venue – the local church for the service and the country setting of Riverside Lodge for the reception.

The venue was going to cost us an arm and a leg, but to save money my kid brother Dan said he'd do the photos. Initially, I'd been a bit dubious about this – he had a habit of catching people unawares. Sometimes, particularly with children and animals, it worked. Sometimes, like that Christmas snap of Uncle Jim picking his nose, or Auntie Irene flashing her knickers, it was just bad taste.

'The Riverside, eh?' Gemma was impressed.

'There was a cancellation earlier,' I said, 'but in the end, we turned it down. Call me superstitious, but I don't fancy the idea of substituting for some couple who've decided to call their wedding off.'

'It doesn't bode well, does it?' Gemma said. 'So, it's September then?' she added

'That's right. You will be my bridesmaid, won't you?'

'Now, that depends,' she said.

'Nothing was ever straightforward with Gemma. That's why I liked her.

'On what?'

I was expecting her to make demands. No peach or aqua, and definitely no puff sleeves, that kind of thing. Gemma was tall, with a straight-up-and-down sort of figure. She looked great in sharp tailoring and block colours, but in anything flowery, frilly or full skirted, she looked like she'd raided her auntie's dressing-up box.

'On whether I'm here or not.'

She was always getting these daft ideas, was Gemma, about throwing in her job at the solicitors' office where she had worked since leaving school. Occasionally, she even got as far as updating her CV. But that's as far as it ever went.

The job was convenient, well paid and relatively undemanding, and she always came to the same conclusion, just as she was at the point of putting in an application for some other job. Better the devil you know, she'd say, and at the end of the day a job was only a job.

'So, where are you thinking of going, then?'

The space between my question and her answer measured the length of a heartbeat. Two at the most. Barely enough time for the thought to flit into my head that she'd entered another one of her restless patches.

But now, more than a year later, when I replay our

conversation in my head, I remember that silence differently. It lengthens, changes texture – thickens and grows heavy. It becomes the difference between yes and no and as final as the difference between then and now.

'I've got cancer, Jo,' she said. 'And it's not the good sort. Not that there's ever a good sort, of course. But you know what I mean.'

She sounded apologetic, as if somehow, she'd let me down. Me with a wedding in the offing and her unable to promise she'd be around to make a show of herself with the best man at the reception. How inconsiderate did that make her?

'Now, don't you dare even think of changing the date,' she said. 'You can book funerals days in advance, but receptions are a different matter altogether.'

Did I tell you about Gemma's morbid sense of humour? It was *her* cancer, she said, when I told her to stop it right there, and as far as she was concerned, that gave her the right to make as many jokes about it as she liked.

Well, fine, I said. But what about me? How was I meant to react to her news? In the end, I took the same journey as everyone else who'd found themselves in my situation. In other words, I boarded the Cliché Bus all the way to Cliché City, passing through Disbelief – 'They've made a mistake, obviously' – and lingering far too long at Rage.

'It's just not fair,' I ranted to anyone who'd listen. 'What kind of a God would allow this to happen to the best friend I ever had?'

The ranting didn't stop at God, either. Nick came in for more than his fair share of stick, too.

'We must be positive,' he said.

'How can Being Positive change anything?' I screamed. 'My best friend is going to die.'

But then I felt ashamed of my selfishness. I had everything to live for. If anyone should be allowed to wallow in self-pity, it was Gemma, not me. Except Gemma didn't wallow. Or if she did, she did it alone.

Of course, despite Gemma's instruction that we should leave everything exactly as it was, I was straight on the phone to Riverside Lodge as soon as the first shock of her announcement had worn off.

A wedding without her as my bridesmaid would be unthinkable, so there was only one thing to do – bring it forward. We'd take the slot that the couple no longer getting married had given up, and superstition be damned. Fate had already done its worst anyway, I told Nick. What else could it throw at us?

Some other pair had got there before us, however, and we were back to square one. The next stop on the journey of grief is Acceptance, so they say. I guess Gemma must have got there quite some time before I did. Patiently, she put up with me rabbiting on about alternative plans. But when I'd finished, she quietly told me that if I did anything to alter them just for her then she wouldn't give her approval.

'We'll get married in four weeks' time,' I said. 'At the registry office. We don't need a reception, but I need you to be there, and to be well enough to enjoy it.'

'No can do,' she said. 'I'm in treatment then. Besides, this is your day, not mine. You'd hate a register office wedding, you know you would.'

Don't you just hate it when your best friend remembers everything you've ever said to her?

'Look, Jo,' she said. 'Please. I mean it. No changes. If I'm there, I'm there. If I'm not, well, I'll still be there, if you see what I mean.'

We both cried then. There was a lot of sobbing – although it was more like howling on my part – and a great deal of hugging. When we came out the other end, things seemed to have changed.

It was as if the rest of the world had retreated. There was just Gemma and me, and though there were these other things, too – her cancer, my wedding – our friendship took precedence, which would triumph over any number of tears.

Was it crazy to do what I did next? Nick said I was being morbid. My mother said I was being unrealistically optimistic. Gemma said I was mad, but then I always had been. If it was what I wanted, then she'd go along with it.

Besides, people had been known to live longer than expected, she grudgingly admitted. Doctors were human beings, not soothsayers. The months she'd been given might very well become years. Either way, she had nothing to lose.

So, we shopped for her dress together. It took a while, as she had to keep cancelling, what with treatment and the bouts of exhaustion that seemed to become more frequent as the weeks passed and the wedding grew closer. But we got there in the end.

'As long as you don't mind altering it every few weeks then I'll wear it at your wedding, just like I promised all those years ago,' she said, the first time she tried it on.

The dress was just right for her. Teal to match her eyes and her fabulous complexion, figure skimming and falling to the ground. The shop held onto it to make a few alterations. A week later, I brought it round to her house, as she hadn't felt up to making the trip to town that day.

'You'll look fabulous,' I said, as I drew it out of the box.

She was just out of hospital after one of her many rounds of treatment. I could see she was making a big effort to look interested. She said if I wanted to leave it behind, she'd try it on later, and she put out a hand to stroke it. That's when I noticed how thin her fingers were.

'Don't look at me like that,' she said. 'Tomorrow I'll feel stronger. Leave the dress with me, and I'll have a fitting then with Mum. I promise.'

How difficult it was to hide my tears. I'd been so looking forward to seeing her in the dress that day. Perhaps I'd already had a premonition that she wouldn't be wearing it on the day of my wedding.

But as if she'd read my mind, she struggled to sit up and speak. 'You'll see me in this dress, Jo, I promise you.'

I had to be content with that.

Gemma rallied for a while. I began to believe she really would make it. Plans gathered apace – flowers, menus, wedding gift lists and guest lists were all in place. My own dress was a simple affair, picked out in the blink of an eye.

I chose it for Nick, who loved me most in jeans and sweatshirts. Anything too showy would have made me think I was just dressing up and more concerned with the event than with the years that lay ahead as a married couple – and hopefully an old married couple.

The week before the dress rehearsal, Gemma took a turn for the worse. I rushed to her bedside. There was something ethereal about her, as if she'd already started on a journey away from those who loved her. Frankly, she was embracing it.

'Don't even think of cancelling,' she said. 'Promise me.'

They were the last words she spoke to me. Just days later, she died. I'd lost my best friend and I was inconsolable. Everyone rallied round, of course. Never mind the expense, my parents said, we should go ahead and cancel.

I was almost convinced they were right. It would be disrespectful to Gemma's parents to hold a day of celebration just days before her funeral. Nick agreed. He muttered something about doing it later – a quieter affair, just us and a couple of witnesses this time.

I almost succumbed. But a phone call from Gemma's mum reminded me of my promise. And so, the wedding went ahead. One year later, much of it's a blur. But it wasn't all sad. There were some happy bits, too.

Walking down the aisle with my dad, whose comforting grip on my arm gave me the confidence I needed to propel myself to the altar, where Nick was waiting for me, handsome in his morning suit, his face brimming with so much love it lifted my heart, was a moment to savour.

I remember making my vows, too, and walking back down the aisle a married woman. Peace filled my heart.

Yes, this is right, I thought, and I silently thanked Gemma for insisting that we went ahead. I'd never believed in ghosts, but standing at the altar, as the vicar spoke his words, I almost felt Gemma's presence, and I definitely sensed her approval.

You make a beautiful bride, Jo, I imagined her saying. Silently, in my heart, I thanked her.

We had a honeymoon of sorts. Romantic Venice, still warm in autumn.

And then, the day after we came home, my brother called. 'I've got the photos back,' he said.

He sounded bashful. It was a tone I recognised from all the years we'd grown up together. He'd screwed up, I was convinced.

'Dan, what have you done?' I was his older, sterner sister again.

'Nothing,' he said, 'The photos are great. Only … there are one or two. Look, perhaps I should just bring them round and you can see them for yourself.'

Laid out on the kitchen table, the story of my wedding unfolded in pictures. Guests milling around, chatting, laughing, joking. Mum smiling through her tears while dad looked proud. Everything you'd expect from your wedding photos – more than I expected from my little brother, if truth were told.

'Hey, these are genius, kid,' I said. 'I take back anything I have ever said about you being a talentless amateur.'

'I'm flattered,' Dan replied. He dipped his hand in his inside pocket and brought out a clutch more snaps. 'Now look at these.'

He made room on the table for the three photographs he'd selected. 'I thought at first it was something in the processing,' he said. 'A smudge or something I'd spilt. But then I looked closer, and I saw . . .'

A fuzzy shape. Standing behind me at the altar. Then at my shoulder, clearer this time, the outline of a figure in a long dress. Then the final shot: an empty church, guests departed. Only the figure remained, the faintest blur, hovering in the aisle.

'Gemma!'

'You think so, too?' Dan said.

I homed in on the photos now, flicking from one to the other, greedy to see more than their blurred images offered up. I was conscious of Dan speaking, excited, tripping over his words, but I was oblivious to all of them. All I could think about was Gemma, and how she'd kept her promise.

If I showed these photos to Nick, what would he say? That a couple of blotchy, botched pictures were what we should have expected from Dan, who was well meaning enough, but no pro?

Or would he, like Dan, like me, think that these weren't blotches but something else altogether? Gemma, keeping her promise to be the bridesmaid at my wedding?

In turn, I pressed each photo to my lips. 'Thank you,' I whispered.

I keep those three photos in my bedside drawer. On our first anniversary, I took them out and looked at them again. Next year, I'll do the same, and every year after that. I'll never forget her. My best friend. My beautiful bridesmaid.

First published 2010, *Fiction Feast*

The Cat on the Mat

Bob always said that if there was such a thing as reincarnation then he would come back as a cat. At the time, Delia had paid this remark scant attention. But if he had intended coming back as anything then, yes, a cat would be it.

In life, Bob had been a hairy man – apart from on his head. His beard was many shades of grey. Granted not 50, but maybe five or six – and there was quite a bit of white in there, too. In a particular kind of light, it was even possible to pick out some flecks of ginger.

He'd been a large man, and a greedy one with it. So, if coming back as a feline had ever been his intention then it would be as a big, fat, long-haired tabby that he'd return. But the cat that sat shivering on her doorstep when she opened the door to put out the empty milk bottle that night was black and skinny and rather pathetic looking.

She shut the door on it immediately, not wanting to give the bedraggled creature any encouragement. Then she came inside and did what she always did now Bob was no longer there to do it. She checked she'd turned off the fire and hadn't left any lights burning, unplugged the kettle and made sure all the doors were locked. Then she took herself off to bed, where she remained resolutely on her side for the rest of the night. They said you knew when you'd come to terms with being widowed when you finally plucked up the courage to sleep in the middle of the bed. Well, she wasn't there yet.

Delia forgot about the cat till next morning, when her bottle of semi-skimmed wasn't on the step where it should have been. Despite still wearing her dressing gown and her slippers, she braved the early morning air and stepped outside to investigate. She saw it immediately. The bottle lay on its side by the privet hedge. The top was off and only a couple of inches of milk remained. Next to it lay a milky stain.

It was obvious what had happened. That wretched cat had stolen her pint and now she was going to have to drink her tea black. As bad starts to her day went, this was pretty much up there with the worst of them. There was no sign of the cat. Not that she was looking for it.

The wind got up in the night and suddenly, the mild autumn everyone had been enjoying became winter. Rain threw itself at the window, waking Delia from her light sleep. She pulled the duvet closer and did her best to go back to sleep, but it was impossible. She thought she could hear wailing.

She lay there for a while and listened until she could bear it no longer. She knew what it was all right. Downstairs she padded, dressing gown wrapped tightly around her, warning herself against making a rod for her own back. She didn't even like cats. But as she opened the front door, she finally considered the one thing she'd been avoiding since first clapping eyes on that black stray. What if it wasn't a cat after all? What if Bob had kept his promise and come back?

He was there on the step. How long had he been there waiting for her to let him in? Bob was always forgetting his key. She'd be in the middle of doing something when that familiar coded peal of the doorbell came. Baking, for instance, her fingers sticky with flour and butter, or at that point in her book when the murderer's identity was about to be revealed. Or worse, upstairs wrestling with a clean duvet cover, her head trapped inside as she struggled to work out which corner was which. It was two short rings followed by a long one. And she had to drop everything and let him in.

"You'd better come in," she said to the cat.

He didn't need asking twice.

Very soon after she'd admitted him to her home, she started calling him Bob. It was the first name that popped into her head and, well, it suited him somehow. She couldn't have got on with Smudge or Sooty or Paws.

Funny how he answered to the name almost from the start. It was as if he'd always been a Bob, even before he'd crossed her threshold. He seemed to know his way around the house, too. Jumped up in Bob's chair like it had always belonged to him. Knew where she kept the tins of salmon. The old Bob had eaten salmon twice a week for as long as he'd lived. Good for his heart, he'd maintained. Well, maybe he'd been right. Since it hadn't been his heart that had killed him.

She couldn't quite remember when she started talking to the creature. It seemed to happen naturally. At first, it was silly things. Did Bob want a drink? Did he need to go outside? Was he hungry, sleepy, a tad too warm? Then she started asking him for his opinion.

What did he make of the new neighbours? Were there too many reality programmes on TV? Who did he think would win *Strictly* this year? He never answered. Just licked his paws and yawned and stretched. It was quite refreshing, actually. The old Bob would have gone on for hours.

After a week, it was as if he'd been there forever. They ate breakfast together, just like the old days.

They'd walk down to the bottom of the garden in tandem to check on the winter brassicas. He'd hover behind her while she cleared the table, exactly as he'd done when in human form. When she turned in at night, he'd be there at the bottom of the bed, waiting for permission to jump up and nestle at her feet.

But after a couple of weeks, the arrangement began to have its drawbacks. For a start, he was eating her out of house and home. Partly this was her own fault. She was well aware of how much she was beginning to indulge him, but Bob couldn't live on salmon alone. Pretty soon she was stocking up with other kinds of fish, and chicken, too.

There was other stuff that began to get to her. Like the way he'd prod at the TV remote with a paw exactly at the point when she was most engrossed in a drama and start flicking through the channels until he found some sport. Or how he'd scratch at the door to be let out just as she'd sat down with a cup of tea and *Loose Women* after a morning spent paying bills. That had been Bob's job when he was alive, so it was something she really struggled with now she had to do it herself.

One morning, she was so fed up with the mound of paperwork that had accumulated over the last few months that she'd turned to Bob the Second and asked him if he could help. His reply had been brutal. Turning up both his nose and his tail, he'd stalked off, leaving her to it. It was as if he hadn't heard her.

Selective deafness was how she described it. Bob had always been good at that.

One evening, she received a phone call from her dearest friend, Mel, who was back in the country after visiting her daughter and grandchildren in Australia. She was ringing to invite Delia to stay that very next week.

She'd be delighted, Delia said. She hadn't been anywhere new in months. Actually, since Bob had moved in, she'd barely been anywhere old, either. These days, she would zip round the supermarket in double-quick time in order to get back to him. It wasn't that she didn't trust him not to wreck the house if she left him alone too long. But once or twice, when she'd had no other choice but to leave him for a whole afternoon, it was as if he'd somehow got it into his head to punish her for not putting him first.

It wasn't as if he didn't know perfectly well what the litter tray was for. And somehow, managing to knock over her favourite vase could have been seen as downright malicious. It was one she'd made herself at her pottery class, and she was very proud of it. Admittedly, it was a tad lopsided, but it was the first thing she'd made, and she would have got better. If only Bob had been a bit more encouraging instead of comparing it to the Leaning Tower of Pisa. She hadn't returned for the second term.

When she put the phone down on Mel, Bob was

there, staring up at her accusingly before shuffling away to a corner, where he began to wash himself furiously. Her heart sank. How could she have forgotten about him? She couldn't possibly leave him here alone for an entire week. She was going to have to ring Mel and put her off.

He only emerged from his corner after she'd reassured him that she would cancel her plans the very next morning. Now he was prancing round the room like he'd just won the lottery. Whereas she felt like a woman defeated.

That night, she refused to let Bob into her bedroom. 'I need some me time,' she told him. He kept up the scratching and pitiful meowing for a good hour or so. But when it was obvious she meant business, he slunk away. She was pretty sure he'd punish her for it later and didn't look forward to coming downstairs in the morning. But when she finally did come down, everything in the house was just how she'd left it, and there had been no toilet accidents, either.

'I suppose you'll be wanting your breakfast,' she said to Bob in a flat voice. Unusually for this time of the day, he was standing by the door.

He was still waiting there when she popped her head round the kitchen door to check why he hadn't followed her.

'OK, then,' she said. 'I'll let you out. And then I'll make that phone call to Mel.'

She was expecting another one of his celebratory dances, but instead he just stood there looking up at her, an oddly sympathetic expression on his face.

She opened the door a bit wider, and he tiptoed outside, throwing her one last backward glance.

'Right, then,' she said once she'd shut the door behind him. 'I'd better get on with it.'

Except she didn't. She'd always been good at procrastinating if it was something she really couldn't bring herself to do. And she really didn't want to ring Mel and cancel her visit.

She took her mind off it by getting stuck into a bit of spring cleaning. At lunchtime, she opened the front door and called Bob's name, but there was no sign of him, so she ate alone. It was quite pleasant, actually, just her and *The Archers*, and a whole sandwich instead of half of one because Bob was such a greedy cat.

He didn't come in for tea, either, and nor did he turn up last thing when she put out the empties. And there was no sign of him next morning, nor the morning after that. She almost felt liberated. Gone was the fishy smell of Bob's dinners and the cat hairs all over her clothes. And in their place was a creeping feeling of relief that she'd never actually got round to making that call after all.

The night before she was due to go away, she decided it really was time to pack her things. It really did look like Bob had gone for good. She went about the task cautiously, still half expecting the cat to appear at the bedroom window, demanding to be let in.

Superstitiously, she thought that if she finished the job before this happened then she would have seen the last of him. She got her head down, concentrating on her task, giving little thought to whether or not she was taking the right shoes or had a warm enough jumper. They had shops in Leeds, which is where Mel lived these days. She could buy whatever she needed clothes-wise there. Bob would say it was a waste of money, of course. He'd never understood about clothes. But then Bob wasn't here. Neither was the other Bob.

Exhausted after her task, she took a long bath then set her alarm clock for 8 o'clock the next morning. It looked like this trip was actually going to happen after all, she thought, as she wandered over to the window to draw the curtains.

It was then she saw Bob. He was sitting on the wall at the bottom of the drive, staring up at the bedroom window.

"Oh," she squealed, and she placed her hand over her heart to stop it thumping.

So much for superstition. They stood there staring at each other for a full minute. She couldn't imagine what Bob was thinking. For her part, she was thinking of nothing at all. Panic had frozen her brain. It was Bob who made the first move. Slowly and deliberately, he raised his paw. It was almost as if he were waving her goodbye. But cats didn't wave, did they?

Awkwardly, feeling foolish, she raised her hand and flapped it back at him, whereupon Bob leapt down from the wall, and, tail raised high in the air, wandered off into the darkness.

That night, for the first time since she'd been widowed, Delia moved over to the middle of the bed and fell instantly asleep till the next morning.

First published 2016, *Woman's Weekly*

Stirred and Shaken

Today, we are mostly making macaroni cheese. The ingredients are as follows: 4 oz macaroni; a lump of cheese – don't worry about the size; half a pint of milk; 1 oz plain flour; 1 oz butter; a teaspoon of mustard, salt and pepper to taste.

Oh, and one eighteen-year-old boy, of the long, lanky variety, who's suddenly realised that if he's going to survive his first term at uni, he'd better learn to cook, and sharpish.

'What's an oz?'

We're standing by the cooker, ready to go. He peers at the recipe in my ancient cookbook. I anticipated a challenge, but of the culinary rather than the linguistic variety.

'An oz is an ounce,' I reply, with saintly patience. 'It's a unit of measurement.'

He shakes his head in disbelief. His attitude

causes me to wonder if we should stop now, before things deteriorate further. But then I realise he has a point. We're going to have to convert everything to grams. Or someone will. No point asking me.

He works it out on his phone. 'One oz equals 28.3495231 grams.'

I can feel myself drifting off, like when the man on *The Money Programme* starts talking about interest rates.

'So, four oz would be – well, four times 28.3495231,' he says.

'We could always use spoons,' I suggest. 'One tablespoon is effectively one ounce.'

We bypass the problem of the macaroni falling off the spoon and spilling onto the floor by measuring out four ounces on my scales. It's cheating, but even Delia cheats.

'Just think of it like this. Four ounces is three-quarters of your *Pokemon* mug.'

He fixes me with a scornful look. 'I'm not taking my *Pokemon* mug to uni,' he splutters.

'You could start a trend. Like Sebastian Flyte and Aloysius.'

Scorn changes to incomprehension. *Brideshead's* probably been off the syllabus for years.

The memory of my son, two feet tall, wearing pyjamas with feet and trailing his own teddy behind him as he makes his sturdy way up to bed, elbows its way to the front of my mind. I hold it there. One second. Two seconds. Then, time to crack on, I tell him. First thing is to cook the macaroni. 'Two minutes less than it says on the packet. You don't want it soggy.'

'Al dente,' the boy says, surprising me. 'Sounds like an Italian stand-up.'

We share a giggle. I explain how, when it's ready, he needs to run cold water over it to halt the cooking process, otherwise it will continue to cook as it remains hot. There is a heat in boys, too. They will grow up. It's useless to think you can keep them small and dependent. Much as sometimes you think you'd like to.

'So, that's why we rest meat and slightly undercook vegetables,' I add. 'Unless you're Gran.'

I give him a friendly dig. Now it's time to make the roux. This is your basic, I tell him. If he can make a roux, he can make so many dishes. A good roux will make a chef of him.

'Bring it on, then!'

'You're doing it, not me. This isn't a demonstration, you know.'

He shrugs, game for anything, but suddenly not so cocky. I know that look. He'll be wearing it when he flies off to uni, leaving us behind. Standing on the edge of things, waiting, watching. Giving himself a little push.

'This is easy,' he says.

He's managed to melt the butter without burning it.

'Make sure you use plain flour.' I watch him tip it in. Boys have such big hands. 'Self-raising causes lumps.'

'And we don't want lumps.'

Right now, there's a lump in my throat the size of an egg.

'That's right,' I say. 'Don't stop stirring. Get this bit right and the rest is a piece of cake.'

'Or a bowl of macaroni. What does roux mean?'

'I don't know. It's French.'

My answer seems to satisfy him. Now it's time to add the milk.

'Not too much all at once, and don't stop stirring!'

'I could be here all day.'

He sighs, bored already.

'You carry on doing that and I'll drain the macaroni.'

I could take over. I suspect he might turn up the heat when I turn my back, burn the bottom of the pan and ruin the resulting sauce. But I've got to trust him. I do trust him. He'll be fine. He's ready for this.

When I turn back from the sink with the cooked, cooled macaroni, I marvel at the thick, glossy sauce burping gently in the pan.

'Brilliant! Take it off the heat, now. Add half your cheese. Season, mustard, stir. That's right. Now, how does it taste?'

He dips in his finger. 'Pretty damn good,' he says.

'Chuck in your macaroni next, mix it all up, turn it out into the dish . . .'

'Ovenproof, naturellement'.

'That's right. A bit more cheese and bung it in the oven for twenty minutes. I'll do that. You start on the washing up.'

'What a team!' he exclaims.

'Except you'll be doing it on your own next time.'

Just when I thought I'd get through this, a tear spills from my eye. Fortunately, he's at the sink and doesn't see.

'I'll be thinking of you when I do, Mum,' he says, as my tear splashes into the sauce.

First published 2011, *Woman's Weekly*

Danny Run Home

Danny had invited her, she reminded herself, checking the directions he'd enclosed in his letter. It was written in the chubby, round handwriting that hadn't changed since he was nine and first attempted joined-up writing. She wasn't forcing this visit on him. It was all there in black and white. Even without referring to it, she could have recited his words by heart.

Dear Mum, I am doing all right. You wouldn't know me. I'm getting fat because I'm eating again. But when I can afford trainers, I am going to start running. It's expensive living in this place but I am learning to manage money, and as I'm not doing the drugs anymore – not even drinking – I should soon be able to run to a pair. LOL at the pun.

It was good that he was getting his sense of humour back. He'd always had the ability to make her laugh, right from the first moment she'd held him in her arms, and he'd fluttered open his long-lashed eyes and fixed her with a challenging stare that seemed to say, *All right then, world, what have you got for me?*

He's made us complete, she used to say to Mark, and Mark would nod proudly in agreement. How she loved it when the three of them walked down the road, Danny in the middle, holding tight onto their hands and squealing *again, again* after each time they swung him up into the air.

Funny, she remembered more about Danny's formative years than she did about either of the other children that followed. First tooth, first steps, first words, first nightmare visit to A&E when he fell off a chair trying to reach the biscuit tin she kept in the cupboard. So many firsts, all locked tightly away in her heart.

There were other firsts, too, of course. First time he wagged school and they got a call from the head. First time he came home with that glazed look in his eyes. First time he didn't come home at all. She'd done a lot of work trying to blot those firsts out.

How to explain Danny as a small boy? She'd been asked to do that once at the support group meeting. She'd gone alone because Mark had point blank refused to go with her.

What was the point? he said. This was Danny's problem. No amount of sitting in a circle on hard chairs and *sharing* would make a scrap of difference to whether he chose to come off the drugs or take so many that one day he'd end up killing himself. He sneered at the word 'sharing'. She should have known then that he wasn't going to be in it for the long haul.

So, she'd gone alone. Just to get out of the house. And to get away from herself. She thought that listening to other people's problems might make her forget her own. And they did for a while, especially when she was put on the spot and asked to talk about her son as he had been, as she'd like to see him again.

'He was an imp,' she said, shyly. 'A scamp. Kind, though. And sensitive. He couldn't bear seeing people bullied. Full of laughter, too.'

Everyone in the group had smiled and nodded, as if in recognition. They must have had sons like that once, too. For a few moments after she'd finished speaking, a stillness lay over them – a communion of like-minded souls. It was as if they believed if they just hoped for it hard enough, they could get those sons back. But of course, they all had to go back home when the meeting was over. And face a very different reality.

During those dark years, opportunities for laughter had been few and far between. There was a time when she didn't think she'd ever laugh again.

'He's squandered every ounce of love we've

poured on him,' Mark said once. 'He's used us both up.'

She'd never forgotten that. Funny word, 'squander'. But no other word could have described Danny's wasted years more accurately.

By rights, she should hate her son for what he'd done to their once tight little unit. His addiction had bred anxiety in the younger two. They'd struggled to thrive in the festering atmosphere of mistrust and anger that gradually began to envelop the home where once they'd felt so safe and secure. There were bitter rows, recriminations. Twice she'd had to break up a fight when Danny pushed his father too far. It wasn't right, bringing kids up in such a place. It wasn't fair on them.

She wondered if they'd believed her when she told them how much they meant to her, even though, during that dreadful period, she knew it must appear she only ever had time for Danny.

Or did they think how unfair it was that they, who'd never put a foot wrong, never stolen money to buy drugs, never broken their mother's heart or made Dad feel ashamed of being their parent, occupied a smaller space in her heart than the boy who'd done all those things, and more?

'You're going to have to choose between your oldest son and the rest of us, Julie,' Mark had said when things got really bad.

He'd had such hopes for his son. What father

didn't? But Danny just wore him down with it all, and those dark circles round his eyes and the lines on his face that seemed to have sprung from nowhere were proof for everyone to see.

Who could blame him for walking away? She didn't, truly, though there were times when she wished he could have found it in himself to be a little stronger – just for her, if not for Danny. But Mark had never possessed much patience, and when Danny was using there was no reasoning with the boy. He was a stranger to them all. And all the love he'd ever felt for his mother, his father, his little sister, Katy, and for his kid brother, Tom, might as well never have existed. He only loved drugs. Hated them, too, of course, when he was coming down from a hit and had no money to buy any more. But that was what his mother's purse was for. And once he'd scored, any loathing he'd ever felt for his habit disappeared as quickly as it took him to hand over the stolen money to whichever skanky dealer he'd managed to get hold of.

She'd called Mark last night. Told him where she was going. Read their son's letter over the phone with pride.

'I'm ready to see you, Mum, at last. I want to prove that I'm on the right road and I've no intentions of wandering off it.'

She'd read his final words with a trembling voice.

'See,' she said. 'He's serious this time. He's never let me visit him before.'

She was on the verge of asking him to come with her. To see the two of them united again – what a lot that would mean to Danny. And how much it would mean to her, to be able to go home and tell Katy and Tom that Dad had made it up with their brother at last. But what he said next stopped her in her tracks.

'Don't read too much into it, love. It's still early days.'

'I might have known you'd say that,' she'd replied, bitterly. She gave him Danny's address anyway.

She wouldn't let Mark infect her with his pessimism. No way. Six months Danny had been clean, and if he could do six months he could do six years, sixteen years, sixty years. He could meet a girl – or a boy – and have a family that he stood by when times got rough. Some men did that. And fortunately, in place of the ones that didn't, there were mothers that remained faithful. There were always mothers.

Here was his road. An ordinary street full of ordinary houses. You wouldn't think, from the outside, that number thirty-two was anything other than a nice family home.

How much did the neighbours know about the people who lived there, each with their own room, a sponsor and a programme that helped them stay clean so that hopefully, in time, they could move on and give up their room to some other poor soul who'd made one bad choice too many?

The people who lived in this street probably had good jobs and clever, well-behaved children. No doubt they saw her son as a loser, a criminal, a junkie. *Poor soul?* They'd laugh in her face.

If they happened to be peering through their net curtains as she walked past today and suspected which house she was visiting, what opinion would they form of her? In their eyes, she was a feckless mother, no doubt, with an equally feckless husband – if she even had a husband. A woman who'd failed miserably at the one thing mothers were supposed to do – teach their children right from wrong.

Goodness knows, she'd thought that way herself in her time. *How can you not know your own child is a junkie? Why don't their parents stop it before it gets out of hand?* She'd sat in the comfort of her sitting room and passed heavy judgement on the desperate families that told their stories to a studio audience on TV. Enjoyed it almost, up there on the moral high ground. But now she knew. And for as long as she lived, she'd never pass judgement on another human soul ever again.

Taking a deep breath, she surveyed the blue door for several moments before ringing the bell. Nothing. *Was it even working?*

She tried again, but even before she removed her finger from the buzzer, she heard footsteps running down the stairs. Nervously, she put a hand to her hair and stroked it. She'd taken a lot of care with her appearance today. But she still worried she wouldn't be up to scratch.

'Mum.'

She hardly recognised him. He'd grown tall, and yes, he was right, he *had* put on a bit of weight. But it suited him. The last time she'd seen him, he'd had an old man's frame, the bones of his face jutting out so sharply that the sight of it pierced her heart. There was colour in his cheeks and life in his eyes once again.

'Can I hug you?' she said.

You had to ask with lads when you were in a public place.

'Course you can. Only not here. Someone might see.'

When she did get to hug him, once they were in his room and she'd taken in its cell-like neatness with one glance, she thought she'd never let him go. He smelled clean again. Healthy. Her little boy. Except he wasn't that. She'd made that mistake before. Protecting him, covering up for him, making excuses for his atrocious behaviour.

'He's his own person,' Mark had reminded her. 'A man, almost. You're doing him no favours treating him the way you do. Being so understanding. Babying the lad.'

He was right, of course. She should have listened

to him. You've got to be cruel to be kind, the saying went. She often wondered, if she had to go through all that again, if she'd do things differently. Probably not. She was stupid like that where her kids were concerned.

He made her tea, chattering all the time. He liked it here. He had mates. Next week, he was going to sign up for college so he could get those GCSEs he mucked up last time.

When he'd run out of things to say, she asked him if he'd consider coming home one day. That was when he faltered. He couldn't. Not yet. Not with all his history. He knew too many people like himself there. Like the way he'd been, he emphasised.

'I'm strong,' he said. 'But I'm not that strong.'

'Of course,' she said. 'But full marks for recognising it.'

Always find something positive to say, they'd told her at the support group. It worked. He sat up straighter, raised his head, stopped fidgeting in his seat. He asked her about Katy and Tom. It was her turn to talk at length then, because as soon as she'd finished one tale, another popped into her head that she must share. And it put off the inevitable. But finally, she'd run out of tales.

'Have you seen Dad?'

The hope in his voice touched her deeply. She smiled, not wanting him to blame himself for Mark walking out on them. 'The kids see him,' she said. 'They're always down there . . . but I don't.'

She couldn't tell him about the phone call, and how Mark had turned down the invitation to come here with her.

'I'm sorry, Mum,' he said. 'For everything.'

She thought he was about to crumble. She saw the signs. She definitely was. So, she started scrabbling in her bag.

'Here,' she said, handing over the box she'd wrapped in Christmas paper, which was all she'd been able to lay her hands on this morning.

'For me?' He took it; surprised, delighted, even before he knew what was inside. He tore off the wrapping and removed the lid from the box.

'Trainers!' He lifted one of them out and held it up to admire it.

She started babbling again. She hoped his feet hadn't grown and they were still the right size. She'd asked the boy in the shop, who'd have been about Danny's age, if it was a brand that would be acceptable to a nineteen-year-old lad, because she knew these things were important. He'd said yes, most definitely, he had a pair like this himself.

While she rabbited on, he kicked off his shoes, exchanging them for the new trainers, tying the bow in that familiar, cack-handed way. He was six again, with his first pair of trainers, his face lit up like Christmas.

'These are brilliant,' he said.

'You told me you were going to take up running,' she reminded him.

He nodded enthusiastically. She pushed to the back of her mind Mark's words.

What are you doing wasting your money on good trainers? He'll only sell them and spend the money on drugs.

'I trust you, Danny,' she said.

He stuck out his legs and stared at his feet, flexing them repeatedly, refusing to look at her. He knew what she meant.

'My bus is due,' she said, suddenly realising the time. 'Will you walk me to the bus stop?'

'Sure. I'll go for a run afterwards. Just a little one to break them in.'

'Sounds like a plan,' she said.

They smiled at each other properly for the first time that afternoon. They'd broken the ice and it felt natural between them. It made her feel so good.

It was pleasant to be walking down the street with her son on a weekday afternoon. They swapped all the jokes they knew, and it was if the bad years just rolled away like a stone from a tomb. She felt properly alive again.

Once or twice, they passed people going the other way. She acknowledged them with a nod and a smile, and they acknowledged her back. One time, they would have looked the other way if she'd passed them in the street with

74

Danny walking next to her. Like despair was contagious.

She wanted to say something meaningful before the bus arrived, but it was already waiting at the corner and the other passengers were getting on, so she had to settle for a quick kiss on the cheek and a promise to text him.

'Thanks for coming, Mum,' he said. 'And thanks for these.'

'You're welcome, son,' she replied.

She had a lump in her throat as she handed over her DayRider for inspection. The driver nodded her on. It was packed downstairs, so rather than stand she made her way to the top deck, which was empty apart from a young man sitting at the back locked into his personal stereo. She'd only just fallen into a seat when the driver lurched forward. They were off.

And there was Danny, on the pavement, running by the side of them, trying to keep up. She opened the window, stuck out her hand and waved madly. He saw her and returned the gesture. But then they turned a corner and left him behind.

She sat back in her seat and began to relive the day. She wished she had someone to talk it over with. She needed to dismantle the afternoon, like Mark did with that motorbike of his. He'd take it apart, inspecting all its dozens of components before reassembling it again, marvelling at how all the bits still fitted together.

Her phone rang. One of the kids, probably, wanting to know when she'd be home. But Mark's name flashed up. What could he want?

'Mark?'

'How was he?' he asked.

'He was fine. I'm on the bus, so . . .'

So, I'm not going into detail, her words implied.

'I've been thinking. His number. Is it still the same? Only, I thought I might . . .'

Her heart rose in her chest and fluttered like a little bird.

'Yes,' she said. 'It's still the same. I've just left him. He's out on a run now. Ring him later.'

'I will.'

'He'd love it if you did, Mark. He was asking after you.'

'Was he?' He sounded pleased. A beat, then: 'What you doing for tea?'

'I hadn't thought. I've not had time to shop today.'

'Then let me take you out. All of you. Just a pizza.' She could sense his nervousness.

'Wouldn't you rather it was just you and the kids?'

Another beat, then: 'No, I want you to come. I want us to be a family again.'

She wanted that, too. It was all she'd ever wanted. But it wasn't so simple. Nothing ever was.

'You let me down, Mark,' she said. 'Walked out on me when I needed you more than I've ever needed you before.'

'I know. And I'm sorry. I was weak and selfish.'

'What's to stop you being weak and selfish again?' she asked him.

Cruel to be kind.

'I'll tell you,' he said. 'You are. And Katy and Tom. And Danny. You're my wife. They're my kids. It's all a man's got in the world. I don't want to be one of those sorts of men anymore.'

There was a lump in her throat that threatened to burst.

'Dealing with Danny . . . it broke me,' he went on. 'It was the only way. I couldn't match your strength. I was ashamed. So, I left.'

She could hold out. Maintain she didn't need him anymore – that she'd done all right without him these last few months. But she hadn't. Not really. He was the man she loved still.

'I'll come,' she said. 'Pick us up round six.'

He let go of a long, long sigh and thanked her, relief flooding his voice. She hadn't realised it, but the bus had been at a standstill throughout most of their conversation. It was rush hour; of course. They could be here for ages.

'Better make that seven at this rate,' she said. 'Traffic jam.'

'Right-o. Looking forward to it.'

Their conversation over, she returned her phone to her bag and stared out of the window. They were out of town now – just – and the wide pavement running alongside the road was empty of pedestrians, except for a young boy with a red face and brand-new trainers pounding the path. Before she could properly register who it was, the bus had gathered speed and they'd left him behind. But not before he'd raised his head to the top deck and seen her. And waved.

First published 2013, *Fiction Feast*

French Onion Soup

It was lunchtime as the coach drew into the sleepy French village of Mont Marchais.

'We have two hours,' bellowed Marion, as the doors slid open. 'Plenty of time to get your fill of the village, and to grab some food.'

Get your fill; grab some food. Each stock phrase that fell out of Marion's mouth confirmed Joyce's suspicion that in the mind of their tour guide, these excursions were simply one damn inconvenience after another.

Ancient monuments, market squares, stunning pastoral scenery – they were irrelevancies to be endured. For Marion, the real purpose of this five-day trip to 'hidden' France was *sitting in the wretched coach.*

'If Marion had her way,' she growled in Eric's ear, 'we wouldn't bother stopping and getting out at all.'

But Eric was negotiating the difficult step down and so had failed to hear her. It hadn't helped that she'd voiced her grumble into his bad ear. Not that his good ear was much better.

Attracted by the smell of food drifting towards them from the row of pavement cafés, tables already full of chattering diners eagerly anticipating lunch, some of the more confident members of their party headed in that direction. Others hung back, waiting for Marion to suggest the name of the restaurant of *her* choice.

'Come on,' Joyce said to Eric, whose feet were already leading him towards Marion and her hangers on. 'You know what'll happen if we stick with the group. We'll end up eating panini or pizza.'

That wasn't her idea of a French lunch at all. Once, it wouldn't have been Eric's, either. Marion's heartiness was very wearing.

Assertiveness tips was the name of the article in the woman's magazine she'd nonchalantly leafed through on their journey across the channel. She'd no idea back then – pre-Marion – just how useful those tips would prove to be.

She was exhausted by the pace they'd been set since arriving. Up at seven to tackle the complications of the French bathroom and the buffet breakfast, which always entailed several trips because Eric could never manage to remember the right cutlery. Then the dash to the coach that left promptly at nine, because, unfortunately, according to Marion, parking restrictions meant there was no pick-up outside the hotel. It was a relief when the coach finally began negotiating the rush-hour traffic out of town, so she could close her eyes for five minutes and try to get her breath back.

Joyce cast another glance at Marion and her coterie, half tempted back. Perhaps it would have been much less nerve-wracking to join them, even if they did end up in a pizza parlour, she mused. Immediately, she changed her mind. Once you surrendered your independence, what did you have left?

For her own sake, she needed to prove she could still look after herself – and Eric too, if need be. Neither of them was quite ready to be parked in a twilight home just yet. Hence the idea of this trip, which had horrified the children.

'Are you sure Dad's up to it, so soon after his stroke?'

'How will you get on hauling your luggage on and off trains? You're both very frail these days.'

On and on it went. As if she needed reminding of the hundred and one things that could go wrong. She lived with Eric. His failing health and his failing memory had become as familiar to her as his breakfast habits.

It was when she caught the word panini that her mind was finally made up. Taking a firm grip on Eric's arm, she voiced her intentions. 'I've had enough of being bullied by that bloody woman,' she said.

Eric suddenly shrank back, his eyes full of bewilderment

'How hard can it be to find our way round this place?' Joyce softened her voice to dispel his anxiety. 'There can't be more than half a dozen streets.'

'Well, if you think so,' he said, reluctantly. 'As long as we don't wander too far.'

She reassured him they wouldn't.

'What time did she say the coach would be leaving?' Eric said.

Joyce sighed inwardly. No sooner had one problem resolved itself than another always seemed to occur to Eric these days. She told him two o'clock, though she wasn't a hundred per cent positive. Perhaps forgetfulness was catching.

Eric stood there, staring at his watch, weighing up the information she was certain he'd have forgotten as soon as they turned the corner. He kept her waiting so long that she began to wonder if he'd decided to throw his lot in with the others and leave her stranded. But in the end his loyalty to her proved stronger.

'Which way?' he said.

'You choose,' she replied.

Not a good idea, she realised, as panic sprang up

in those cloudy eyes, once so clear and sharp and blue. Eric had been so decisive as a young man. Once upon a time, he had led, and she had followed. Now, increasingly, their roles were becoming reversed.

'We'll find a nice café,' she said, squeezing his hand. 'And we'll have a proper lunch, with wine and coffee and the plat du jour.'

'None of your panini,' he chuckled, squeezing back.

When he joked with her, she almost convinced herself things were back to how they'd been before the stroke that had affected his mobility and the ensuing confusion which hadn't – as the doctors said it might – resolved itself.

Instead, it had got worse, so that these days their conversations went round and round in one long, continual, exhausting loop. Occasionally, she dared to broach a new, unfamiliar topic. Recently, for example, she'd mentioned their grandson James's acceptance at university. It had proved a complete waste of time. As far as Eric was concerned, James was a boy of twelve, who loved football and hated sprouts and could never get the hang of simultaneous equations. It seemed far simpler not to disillusion him.

'It's a pretty village,' Eric said. 'What's it called again?'

Joyce had turned off the main street, all the better to get away from Marion, though her hearty voice still pursued them even when she was out of sight.

'Mont Marchais,' she said, for the third time today.

'Have we been here before? I know we've been to Paris and, er . . . those other places. But I don't know about here.'

'No,' she said. 'Not here. But we've been to plenty of little villages like it.'

Eric chuckled. 'That's right,' he said, his face suddenly relaxing. 'We came camping, didn't we? Patsy was always sick in the car.'

'Happy days, eh, Eric?'

The first time they'd been to France had been on their honeymoon. Seven days in Paris. Joyce had been a nervous bride, terrified of inflicting her schoolgirl French on the natives. By contrast, Eric had taken the whole experience in his stride, ordering from the menu anything that sounded as remote from English food as it could be.

After that first time, France had become 'their place'. Every summer, they returned, taking the car over on the ferry. When their youngest, Patsy – now a matronly forty-six – decided she'd had enough of schlepping round France with the wrinklies, they'd still kept it up. France meant far too much for them to break the ties. Although they'd never have deserted England to set up home there. If France was a love affair, then England was a marriage.

Eric's health problems had put an end to thoughts of travel. This was their first time back in three years.

So far, it hadn't been a resounding success. But Joyce was ever hopeful.

There were brief moments, when they were on their own, when she was able to blot out all thoughts of the coach and of Marion and her galloping commentaries and imagine they were independent travellers again, in charge of their own destinies, just as they'd been when they were young, before crabbed old age set in.

They'd arrived at a ramshackle looking restaurant set halfway down the quiet, cobbled street, finally out of reach of Marion's strident voice. The entire row of long, slim buildings leaned in on one another, like a line of decrepit neighbours stoically propping each other up. Old they may have been, yet there was a sort of elegance about them, too.

'Let's try this one.' Joyce pointed to the sign a short distance away above their heads, rattling back and forth in the warm breeze.

'Henri's. Now that's French enough for me.'

The fluttering awning over the entrance beckoned them in. Most of the tables were taken, which was a relief to Joyce. She'd been in a couple of situations with Eric recently, when the family had taken them out, where he'd insisted on changing their table half a dozen times at least, because something or other hadn't suited him.

The children had been beautifully patient with him, but she'd been mortified by the curious looks they got from the rest of the diners – not to mention the barely concealed hostile ones from some of the waiters – and she'd rather not have to go through any of that when she was alone with him. Especially not here, in a foreign country.

'So, Eric. What do you think?' she said, once they'd been seated and presented with the menu.

She liked the idea of the salade au chèvre chaud to start followed by the lapin au four. She was hungry, and she hoped she wasn't going to have to take Eric through every item before he settled on something. At the back of her mind was Marion, their very own winged chariot, who could not be kept waiting.

But thankfully, Eric had already made up his mind.

'Onion soup,' he said. 'Steak hâché. Frites. Remember?'

Joyce glanced at him over her menu, puzzled. Perhaps a small glass of wine each, then, rather than the bottle she'd envisaged. The pavements were uneven, and they didn't want any accidents. Besides, Eric's face, feverishly lit up as he rattled off his choices, might just be a cause for concern.

'You wore a blue dress,' he continued. 'And those high heels. At the table you took them off because your poor feet were aching so much. Then you put them in my lap, and I massaged them between courses.'

Joyce let out a stifled squeak, her hand flying to her mouth. Eric was talking about their honeymoon.

That second night, after they'd walked around all day, exploring the sights. They were both ravenous and should have been tired. Yet they were beyond exhaustion, feverish with passion and high on love.

'You remember that? From all those years ago?'

'You had a blister on your heel. Neither of us knew the French for plaster. Still don't.'

Eric let out a hoot of laughter, drawing glances from one or two of the other tables. Joyce groped for Eric's hand, squeezing it tightly. Let them stare, she thought.

'Now you say it, I remember it, too,' she said, softly.

A tiny bistro, somewhere on the Left Bank. Candle lit, to hide the shabby walls and to complement the haggard faces of the older diners, they agreed. That overwhelming pungent smell of garlic. A chanteuse singing of love and loss. Tears sprang to Joyce's eyes, and she tasted salt.

'What else do you remember about that night?' she said.

Eric stared into the distance, concentrating hard. It was as if he were observing the young couple they'd once been.

'I remember the envious glances because I was with the most beautiful girl in the restaurant,' he said. 'And thinking how lucky I was to have met you, and how much more meaningful my life was going to be now that we were married.'

'Oh, Eric.'

Joyce was suddenly overwhelmed with a girlish coyness she hadn't felt in years.

'It's been a good marriage, hasn't it, Joyce?'

'It's been wonderful, Eric.'

She was aware of the waitress hovering at her elbow. Eric continued talking, oblivious. 'Although it's been a bit tricky recently,' he said.

She squeezed his hand again. 'We'll get through it,' she said. 'We've got each other, remember that!'

'Are you ready to order?' The waitress spoke in fractured English, addressing her question to Joyce, who threw it back at Eric. 'You do it, Eric. Tell the waitress what we're having.'

Confidently, he read from the menu. Just like that time all those years ago, his voice strong, his accent so bad it was touching. 'Soupe a l'oignon. Steak haché. Frites. Deux fois, s'il vous plaît. Et deux verres du vin rouge.'

'D'accord, monsieur,' the waitress said, with a pretty smile.

'You did that perfectly, Eric,' Joyce said when she had gone.

'When do we have to be back at the coach?' Eric asked her.

Joyce sighed. She'd almost forgotten Marion's three-line whip.

'Let's not worry about that just yet, dear,' she said.

'We'll just enjoy our meal, shall we, then we'll have a little wander back.'

'Let them eat panini, eh?' Eric chuckled, as the waitress returned with their wine.

First published 2010, *Woman's Weekly*

Paper Cut

When the letter came announcing that Janice had been accepted at the grammar school, Jack Crump celebrated by spending the afternoon in The Dog, announcing to all and sundry that, of course, his daughter got her brains from him.

The regulars were polite enough to refrain from asking why, if that were the case, he was a brickie and not a billionaire. Nor were they cruel enough to suggest it was more likely his missus the girl had got her brains from.

After all, Sheila Crump had clearly had a massive brainwave the day she decided to run off with a man who could offer her a better life than the one her feckless husband provided for her. But the locals at The Dog had too much fondness for Jack Crump to spoil his red-letter day. They were generous in their congratulations, even when he'd reached his sixth pint and started getting maudlin. It might be their habit, after a couple of drinks, to look back wistfully at their bachelor days and wish themselves there again, but it was all talk. They wouldn't have swapped Jack's sorry single life for their own no matter what.

By contrast, the day the postman brought the letter that was – hopefully – to alter the course of young Janice's life forever, Mary Crump, her aunty, spent most of it worrying her way through several mugs of strong, brown tea and a week's supply of broken biscuits (one of the perks of her job at the biscuit factory), wondering how on earth they were going to afford the uniform.

Janice Crump did a bit of both. She celebrated the fact that at long last she could get away from all those people who'd blighted her life for so long. Like Gary Openshaw, who didn't know what a hanky was for, and Brenda Blears, who still counted on her fingers and moved her lips when she did silent reading. Not to mention Michael Black, whose dad was in prison, and who – according to her Aunty Mary – was heading the same way himself. And that was just to start with.

At grammar school it would be different. White handkerchiefs (six, embroidered with initials, black) were items on the uniform list, so there'd be no need for runny noses, and everyone would be able to read fluently. The girls who went there were all nice, bright girls, so her teacher said. From good homes.

It was this last point that worried Janice. She

couldn't help wondering what they would think of her. Was she from a good home? She somehow didn't think so. For a start, they were poor.

People in books were poor, but in Janice's experience, it was a different kind of poor. For one thing, it was altogether more temporary and infinitely more reversible. And no matter how impoverished these fictional families were, they still resided in huge – albeit draughty – houses and had the wherewithal to support at least one trusty retainer who could be relied on to devote themselves to the domestic side of things while the main characters got on with the important business of reclaiming their rightful inheritance.

'Janice is an avid reader' had been written on her report since infant school, so she knew what she was talking about. If the carpet in the living room was threadbare and the curtains frayed, and if some weeks they had to hide upstairs and stay quiet when the rent man came, it didn't take from the one thing that Janice's house possessed in abundance – books.

It was in books that she had taken refuge when she realised her mother would never be coming back. (It was also in books that Sheila Crump had recaptured the romance that had flown out the window when poverty slipped in over the threshold Jack had carried her over on their wedding day. From there, it was but a short step to translating her fictional yearnings to reality, in the form of Stanley

Horton, a travelling salesman to whom she lost her heart and who later broke it when he made it plain that in his line of business, there was no room for kiddies.)

It was in the books that Janice read how there'd be a hard-working, pipe-smoking father in the background and a mother with a fresh apron and floury hands. If the mother was absent, it was always through death, never desertion. In none of the books she'd read was there a mother who'd run away from home, and who was never mentioned except in hushed tones.

And as for fathers – well, in all the books she'd ever read, there was never one remotely like her own, who'd lost job after job because he couldn't or wouldn't get out of bed some days, or on the odd occasion he did manage to complete a week's work, would blow his wages in the pub, drinking till he could no longer stand.

Then there was Aunty Mary, with her 'nerves'. Not the patrician nerves of literary heroines, with their hour-glass figures, raven, waist-length curls and aptitude for swooning whenever a manly hero strode by. Aunty Mary's nerves sent her scurrying to the biscuit tin, and any man who attempted to sweep her off the lino and into his arms would have to make sure he had a couple of friends on standby (preferably weightlifters) to give him a hand.

The fact was – and it pained her to think this way

– Janice Crump was ashamed of her family. It didn't matter that people down her own street sniggered when they walked behind Aunty Mary as she waddled by. They sniggered at their own fat aunties just as much, and Janice happily sniggered along with them.

She was untroubled by the looks of pity she got from Miss when Michael Black brought up the subject of her mother's flight in maths one morning. She knew for a fact that Michael Black's home life was even more dire than her own.

The difference was that people round here knew her and she knew them – their history, their foibles, their criminal records, the lot. But how would she fare in the middle of all those girls from refined families, who owned their own houses (unlike the Crumps, who rented from the council and had a little black notebook full of sums and red scrawly writing to prove it), who had fridges and even cars, and whose TV stayed put instead of disappearing at regular intervals whenever they failed to meet the payments on the never-never?

There was only one thing for it, she decided, as the start of the new school year approached. She was going to have to reinvent herself. After all, no one from her class would be going with her to grammar school. She was the only girl from her school to be offered a place – the only one from the whole of her estate, as far as she knew. Billy Eckersley and Miles Jackson had both passed the eleven-plus, too, but they'd be going to the boys' school at the other end of town, so the chance of her bumping into either of them was remote.

So, it was armed with this hard thought-out strategy that Janice – clad in the maroon uniform that did nothing for her pale complexion, and her black shoes a size too big to give her plenty of growing room – set out that first day on a mission to introduce Janice Crump, Mark Two to her new classmates.

This Janice Crump had a father who worked in an office, a mother who stayed at home and baked cakes and a maiden aunt whose fiancé had died in combat many years ago, leaving her broken-hearted. It went without saying that Janice Crump, Mark Two lived in a semi-detached, centrally heated, comfortable house with all the mod cons. It worked a treat.

She had a bit of a scare when she thought she recognised a girl from Gladstone Street sitting on her own at registration on that first morning. Gladstone Street was every bit as grim as her own – in fact, it was an exact replica of every other street on the estate.

When the girl smiled, Janice very nearly smiled back and was only saved by Miss Titherington, her new form mistress, instructing the class to *look this way*. For the rest of the morning, Janice contrived to sit as far away as possible from the girl and made a point of looking straight ahead whenever she suspected she might be under scrutiny.

When, during break, Alison Gray and Jane Barker introduced themselves to Janice in the playground and then asked her to sit with them at dinnertime, Janice was ecstatic. Within a week, they were a threesome, inseparable between the hours of nine and three-thirty, when Alison's glossy-haired, high-heeled mother – who worked part-time in the school office – would whisk both Alison and Jane home to the right-side of the tracks and Janice would tramp back alone to her own house in the opposite direction.

Of the two girls, Alison was the one that Janice admired the most. She was tall and slim, and the colour of her skin was golden, even in late autumn. She had a plait down her back all the colours of blonde that had ever existed, and her eyes were green and almond-shaped, like those of the bored cat Janice passed every morning on her way to school.

Jane had a plait, too, but hers was squat and mousey, rather like herself, in fact. Janice didn't really like Jane, but she knew that if she wanted Alison for a friend, then she'd just have to put up with Jane. When she and Alison were alone, Janice experienced the sensation that together they were in a very private club. But as soon as Jane appeared on the scene, she sensed Alison's loyalty shifting. It happened by such slow degrees that Janice could never work out how the shift had actually occurred.

Suddenly, Jane and Alison would be laughing about something that had happened at Guides the previous evening, or reliving what they'd done together at the weekend, and Janice would be floundering on the edge of their friendship, skirting around for a foothold upon which she could hoist herself back into their midst.

There was one way she could make herself the centre of attention again, however. She could make them laugh. One waspish comment about the size of Miss Titherington's rear, or the warble in Miss William's voice whenever she came to a sad bit in *The Children of the New Forest*, which was their class reader, and she was soon back in the thick of things.

But as time passed, it became more of a strain to think up witty and wicked things to say about the staff, and even when she could come up with something, she didn't always feel happy with herself for being so libellous. The teachers were nice to her and would probably have been horrified to find themselves at the butt of her jokes. But her friendship with Alison and Jane was at stake, so she decided she had no choice. And in desperation, whenever Alison and Jane seemed to be edging her out – and Janice couldn't help thinking this was happening more and more often as they neared half term – she took to taking a pop at some of the girls she knew her new friends didn't like.

Alison and Jane fell over each other when Janice imitated Moira Tyson's duck-like walk. They hooted when she did an impression of Iris Townsend's mouse-like voice. And the more they showed their appreciation, the greater the lengths she went to. If her conscience pricked occasionally, for example, the time she reduced Moira Tyson to tears with her impersonation, she ignored it. Moira Tyson was a bore anyway.

On the last day before half term, Janice was heading homeward. Today, her footsteps dragged a little. She didn't feel right; there was a sick feeling inside her stomach that wouldn't let her go, no matter how hard she pretended to ignore it.

Head down, shoulders dragging, she weaved her way through the back streets that led to her estate. The events that had taken place just before the bell rang to signal the end of another week kept playing in her head like a record on automatic.

She couldn't stop thinking about the words Alison and Jane had exchanged when all three of them were coming out of PE. *That girl, Gillian Martin, lives on a council estate, did you know?* Jane had sniggered and Alison had made a grimace and muttered, *Dead common. I thought there was a smell.*

They'd both laughed then and, of course, Janice had joined in. But something had started to shrivel up inside her as she did so, and when her friends waved a casual goodbye before clambering into Alison's mother's car, she suddenly felt bereft. Watching them drive off, she didn't think she'd imagined the contemptuous sneer that Jane had sent her through the back window, a gleeful Alison looking on in apparent appreciation of her friend's nerve.

She heard footsteps behind her, and someone was calling her name. It was Gillian Martin, the girl from Gladstone Street.

'What do you want?' she said, surprised at herself for how easily she could slip out of her new accent and back into her old one.

Gillian wasn't offended by Janice's initial greeting. On Gladstone Street, where 'Who knitted your face and dropped a stitch?' was the customary way to greet someone who had the temerity to hold your gaze for too long, Janice's words would have been considered the very model of politeness.

'I want to warn you,' the girl said.

'Oh, yeah?' Janice hoiked her satchel further up onto her shoulder and kept on walking.

'I've heard them talking about you,' Gillian went on, not in the least bit daunted.

'Who?' Janice asked.

She had a pretty good idea of the answer already, but she was just stalling for time.

'Why do you want to be friends with those two snobs anyway?' Gillian persisted. 'Are you ashamed of where you come from?'

Janice walked faster and began to lose Gillian. Her heart was thudding, and she tried to shut out Gillian's words.

'I'm only telling you for your own good,' the girl

called out. 'They're no better than us, whatever they might think.'

Gillian had stopped walking now but continued to shout her message down the thankfully deserted street, a black speck on the horizon.

'They know all about you, you know. That Alison's mum has access to all the information she wants in her fancy filing cabinet, and she'll have passed it onto Alison,' she yelled.

Janice felt the blood ringing in her ears. It was almost loud enough to shut out the sound of Gillian's voice. Almost, but not quite.

'They're playing with you, Janice. They have been from the start, but you were too dopey to see it. They're going to drop you. Soon. They only want to see you cry. I'm only telling you for your own good.'

Janice quickened her pace into a run and didn't stop till she got to her house. It was a relief that no one was at home to question why her face was streaked with tears and she was out of breath. She threw herself down onto a chair and hugged herself tight to stop herself shaking.

Why do you want to be friends with those two snobs anyway?

Gillian's words rang in her head. She wished she knew how to answer them. Was it because they belonged to a different world from the one she inhabited? A world where nothing was certain except the knowledge that your mum loved someone else more than she loved you and your dad rolled in drunk every Friday night? Was it because when she was with them, she could forget all that and be her new, reinvented self?

All weekend, Janice dragged herself around the house, barely able to speak to anyone. There were nine whole days to get through before she had to face Alison and Jane again. What was it Gillian had shouted after her, as Janice had taken to her toes, not wanting to hear any more? Something about Alison's mum having access to her details in her fancy filing cabinet, which she was bound to have passed onto Alison.

That meant they'd known her address all along – known she lived on one of the roughest estates in town. Known too that her next of kin was her father, whose occupation was 'brickie', and that in case of emergency her aunty could be contacted at the biscuit factory.

They'd known all that and said nothing, listening instead to her lies about her daddy and mummy and her pet poodle, Flash, and the big house she lived in that had gold taps in the bathroom and a garden so big they needed a gardener to help keep it under control.

And why? So that they could rub her nose in her lies when she got back to school, spread it round, tell the whole school what a fibber she was, turn them all against her, then simply drop her, exactly as if she'd never been their friend. *So that they can make you cry,* Gillian had said.

As a rule, Janice had mixed feelings about the weekend. She liked the lie-ins and she looked forward to her Saturday trip to the library. But the other stuff – the chores and the shopping she shared with Aunty Mary – were less thrilling.

This weekend, though, everything was reversed. She couldn't concentrate in the library and found the hushed atmosphere oppressive. After half an hour of searching through the shelves, she left without a single book.

She wanted to be home in her front room, pushing the vacuum cleaner round, ordering her father from chair to chair while she attacked the dust at his feet and he sighed and pretended to be cross with her. Or at the market, meekly trotting behind Aunty Mary, who was on first name terms with all the stallholders and who stopped for a chat with each one of them while Janice chafed at her arm for her to get a move on. She wanted to feel safe, and it was only with her dad or Aunty Mary that feeling safe was a possibility now.

Making her way down the library steps empty handed, she decided to see if she could find Aunty Mary at the market. It suddenly occurred to her, not without some guilt, that with every week that had passed since she'd started grammar school, she'd done less and less to help in the house, insisting that her schoolwork came first. If Aunty Mary felt left out of Janice's new routine, she'd never grumbled but simply continued to struggle round the market on her own with her heavy bags.

Likewise, her dad had taken on her Saturday morning chores, without any complaints. On the contrary, he'd slipped her a half crown piece and told her to take herself to *Woolworths* for some sweets. She deserved a treat, he said, for working so hard all week long.

Where had he got the money from? Last night, he'd stayed in and listened to the radio instead of going to the pub. Come to think of it, last night wasn't the first Friday night he'd been around. Aunty Mary had said something about him doing well, and he'd said something back about it getting easier, but she hadn't really been listening. She'd been too wrapped up in her own problems.

He'd wanted to hear about her week, but she'd said there was nothing to tell. His face had fallen but he'd said nothing, just gone back to his paper. Before she'd started at the grammar school, she'd told them everything, her Aunty Mary had said. She's growing up, her dad had replied. It happens.

Where had she been all this time, Janice asked herself, while her dad was getting sober and her Aunty Mary had been missing her chatter? *Pretending they don't exist,* came the answer. *Denying them, like Peter and the cock that crowed three times.*

The market clock said eleven, and there was Aunty Mary, haggling over a bunch of bananas at the greengrocer's stall. Janice's insides lit up with pleasure at seeing her there, fat and crumpled though she was. What was to be so ashamed of anyway? Her weight, the fact she spoke with a strong accent and worked in a biscuit factory?

What about all the other stuff she did? She didn't have to live with them and wash Janice's clothes and look after her father. She could have run off, like her mother had. But she never had, and she never would.

'What are you doing here?'

Aunty Mary's curt words belied the expression of delight on her face.

'I've come to help,' she said. 'I was at the library but there was nothing I hadn't read.'

'Here y'are, then.' Aunty Mary handed Janice a bag of potatoes.

The first day back after the holidays, she was going to have to face Alison and Jane. She imagined Alison patting the empty seat next to her, inviting her to sit down, then, as soon as Janice made a move towards her, slapping her satchel on it and saying the seat was taken.

It was what girls did when they'd decided they didn't want you to be their friend anymore. She'd done it herself. It was cruel and humiliating and she wished she'd never done it, nor any of those other awful things she'd done to Moira, Iris, and the rest. She wondered if Gillian Martin had a spare seat next to her. She should say thank you to her for what she'd done. She hadn't liked it much at the time, but all the same. *I'm only telling you for your own good. They're no better than us, you know.*

'Happen it's time to leave the children's books behind and start reading the adult ones,' said Aunty Mary, as they weaved their way home through the Saturday morning shoppers.

'Happen,' Janice replied.

She could have said 'perhaps' or 'maybe'. Grammar school words. But right now, she didn't feel like it.

First published 2006, *Woman's Weekly*

Home and Away

Seth had already called out his usual home-from-work greeting, but there'd been no reply, so he shrugged off his jacket and wandered into the kitchen. He found her sitting on the floor by the dryer, surrounded by a heap of laundry. His first thought was that she resembled a beautiful mermaid borne aloft by billowing waves. The sweep of her jaw and the curve of her cheekbones provoked in him a desire to reach out and touch her. But he held back so as not to break the spell.

He didn't often get the chance to contemplate Helen without her noticing, and now he savoured it. When had she lost all that baby weight he'd got so used to hearing her complain about? And when had her hair got so long? Usually, she wore it pulled back to prevent Olly from tugging at it. But tonight, she wore it loose, like she did all those years ago when they'd first met. She'd been talking about getting it cut for weeks, but there was never the opportunity. Maybe she'd finally get round to it when Olly started nursery, she'd say. She'd laugh then, in order not to make him feel bad for working such long hours and making it so difficult for her to get any time to herself.

Olly was one now. They loved him, of course they did, and it had always been their plan to have two. But it was the timing that was all wrong, happening just as Helen had started talking about putting out feelers for freelance work that would fit around childcare.

But with Olly's arrival, she'd put her ambitions to one side. She didn't mind, she said. The kids came first. They were babies for such a short time. Just look at Sara. Why, she'd barely turned round and here she was – five years old, riding a two-wheeler and at school already. Where had all that time gone?

The first time he'd caught her eye, she'd been stressed to the eyeballs. Juggling, as usual. This afternoon it was the shopping bags and Oliver, who was stiff with screaming fury at being harnessed in his car seat, plus the urgency of getting to school to pick Sara up with only ten minutes left before the end of the school day.

'Let me give you a hand with those,' he'd said.

He spoke with the resonant voice of an actor, and he had an actor's looks and style. Not as tall as Seth, but then who was? Slim, thin lipped, which she'd always loved in a man. His leather jacket was shabbily expensive, and he had a scarf knotted round his neck in a casual way that suggested the way he looked was important to him. She'd always said that men who cared about their appearance weren't her type, or else why would she have gone for Seth?

But today he'd caught her stuck slap bang in the middle of the kind of life she'd always said she'd never have. Love was a trap; she was convinced of it. It lured you in with wedding dresses, honeymoons and baby scans. Then it turned the key and ran off, clutching not just your dreams but your entire personality, too. What you got in exchange were dirty floors, piles of laundry, a grumpy husband and kids whose sole purpose in life was to ensure their own survival, even if it came at the expense of your own.

So, just for a moment, as her eyes met those of this chivalrous stranger, who picked up the oranges that had rolled away and returned them to her bag, and who'd placed the rest of her shopping in her boot and then closed it for her, something changed in her. Two minutes, that was the full length of their exchange. But the memory of it stayed with her for the rest of the journey to school, so that even Oliver's wails failed to connect with that switch inside her, the one that usually turned up her nerves to jangling in seconds. When there were tears at the school gate because Mummy had forgotten to buy her favourite snack, she dealt with Sara's tantrum with the sort of equilibrium she'd previously only been able to imagine.

The rest of the evening had been a breeze, too. Those routine jobs – the putting away of the toys, the bedtime negotiations – came and went without leaving a mark on her tonight. And then, when peace finally descended on their little house, with the kids safely asleep, she hadn't minded at all that Seth, who'd taken charge of the remote control then immediately fallen asleep, had slept until bedtime.

All evening, she'd been carrying the memory of that afternoon's brief encounter like a gift. Now, in the middle of a silence only occasionally punctuated by Seth's snores, the moment had come to unwrap it and savour its contents.

When had they begun, these momentary absences of hers? She could be riffling through a drawer searching for an item of clothing – Dylan's tiny socks or Sara's clean vest – but then she'd suddenly stop, and he'd catch her staring at the contents of the drawer, lost in her own little world. Or she'd be chopping onions for dinner, slowly, methodically, seemingly oblivious to everything going on around her. One time, Dylan pulled himself up to stand next to her while Sara clambered on a chair for the forbidden biscuit tin. If she'd fallen down, if Dylan had taken a tumble and bumped his head, would Helen have even noticed?

Now she stood in front of the fridge, gripping the handle. The fridge door was open, and she was staring into it, that faraway expression he'd glimpsed so many times these last few weeks back on her face.

'What are you looking for in there?' Seth said.

She glanced up at him, her face illuminated by the light coming from the fridge's interior, making her look like one of those paintings by the Dutch masters. It was as if she were looking at a stranger, not the man she'd sworn undying love for, the one she'd often run towards on his return from work, as soon as she heard his key turn in the door. When had she done that last? And what was it that had made her stop?

'Mmmm?' she said.

He asked her again. She let go of the handle. The fridge door gave a shiver and a burp before it banged shut.

'D'you know,' she sighed, 'I've completely forgotten.'

She laughed, tilting her head in that way she had. It couldn't have been important, she said. Whatever it was would come back to her. Then she wandered off into the other room, leaving nothing but her scent behind. It was a perfume he didn't recognise. Sultry, sensual, flirtatious. The kind of perfume a woman might wear for a lover.

* * *

She hadn't thought she'd see him again. If he was a man of routine, then maybe – if she went back on the same day and at the same time – she'd catch him in the supermarket car park once more. Did she dare retrace her steps? Another woman, one more adventurous than she, wouldn't give up so easily. She imagined the two of them catching each other's eye once more across a half-empty car park. Would he even recognise her again? And if he did, would he bother stopping in his tracks and coming over to say hi? How would she react? With a smile? Or with some flippant remark about how they couldn't continue meeting like this?

Just the thought of such a close encounter sent an explosion of heat firing through every part of her body. She practised a flirtatious smile, a toss of the hair. How did other women do it – play these romantic games? She'd never known how. She started going to other supermarkets instead of the regular one. She couldn't risk seeing him again. Not because she didn't want to. But because she did.

'These own brand biscuits are nicer than our usual,' Seth said one night, as they sat in front of the TV.

'Different supermarket,' she said.

'What, not another one!' He dunked his ginger biscuit in his tea. It wobbled but remained attached to the bit in his hand. 'I make that three in as many weeks,' he said.

'Variety is the spice of life,' she'd retorted. 'Isn't that what people say?'

He hadn't replied. Just taken another biscuit and stared at it for a long time, ruminating on it before taking a bite.

'You eat too many of those damn things,' she grumbled. 'You'll be getting fat if you don't watch it.'

'Maybe,' he said. And that was all.

He didn't finish the second biscuit, she noticed.

A man who loves his wife doesn't keep her trapped like a caged bird. Once she's stopped singing, if he loves her, he has no choice but to open the cage door and watch her fly away. All he could do was hope she'd come back because she loved him. And if she didn't? He hadn't quite got that far in his imagining. It was far too terrifying.

He'd expected at least some small attempt at refusal on her part when he suggested she took Saturday morning for herself to go and do whatever she wanted, while he stayed home and looked after the kids. But there'd been none.

'That's brilliant,' was what she'd said instead, before immediately rushing off to make an appointment at the hairdressers.

He resented her for finding it so easy to leave. And he loathed himself for the way he felt. Enough to add to his suffering by encouraging her to stay out longer. Get your nails done, he suggested. Go and have a coffee somewhere. Take a trip round the shops afterwards. It's been a long time since you bought something for yourself that wasn't breast pads. So, he only had himself to blame for what might happen next.

She admired her reflection in the glass door of the coffee shop before going inside. The new style made her look both younger and more sophisticated, and she wondered how that was possible. She'd promised Seth she'd treat herself to a coffee before she came home, but if she was going to take him up on his other suggestion – the one about looking round the shops, too – then she was going to have to get a move on.

She spotted him immediately. Sitting on his own in a corner seat. Same jacket, but this time hung carelessly over the back of his chair. The blue of his sweater matched his eyes, which were staring straight back at her over his copy of *The Guardian*. There was no sign of the scarf today. He lowered his newspaper, smiled at her. She smiled back, a hesitant smile, but a smile nonetheless. When he half stood up and pointed to the seat opposite, she felt she had no choice. It would be rude, wouldn't it, to turn away?

* * *

She'd been gone all morning. It was nearly one o'clock now. How long did it take to get your hair cut and coloured? He should have asked. But what kind of man asks his wife when she'll be back from her first free morning in practically a year? The jealous kind. The controlling kind. He wasn't one of those men, was he?

* * *

To get to his table was a matter of a dozen steps at most. But where else would those steps lead? Lovers had clandestine meetings in bars. They snatched moments in hotel rooms on rainy afternoons. They taught each other how to tell lies.

She thought of Seth as she had left him, dressed in his old tracky bottoms and an ancient t-shirt. He'd been feeding Olly. Olly, shrieking with delight, banged the palms of his hands repeatedly on his highchair table, excited at the prospect of more food. The last thing she'd witnessed as she'd closed the door behind her was Seth, the spoon poised in his hand, making aeroplane noises before he directed it into Olly's appreciative little mouth.

How long had she been standing there, refusing to respond to his beckoning?

He was standing in front of her now, raising his voice to make himself heard above the Saturday morning chatter and the cool blue sounds of a tune she remembered. The Eagles. *Lying Eyes*. Appropriate.

'I thought it was you,' he said. He was studying her new hairstyle. 'But then the hair confused me.'

She put her hand to her head. She'd taken Seth's advice and had her nails done, too. Scarlet.

'I've just had it cut,' she said.

'It's lovely,' he replied, his gaze lingering on her face.

She felt her face colour. She'd forgotten what it was like to be admired. Sometimes, she caught Seth watching her. It was always comforting to think he still enjoyed looking at her. These days, she only looked at him in order to criticise. That swipe she'd taken at him the other night, about his weight. It was cruel. She wasn't the only one to have been tired. Seth worked long hours, and he did it all for them.

'No baby today,' he said, his words breaking into her thoughts.

'Olly's with his daddy,' she said. 'My husband.'

His smile faltered, then returned. She felt awkward, wondering why she'd felt it necessary to mention she had a husband. Wasn't her wedding ring proof enough of that?

'Then perhaps you've got time to have a coffee?'

He wore a ring, too, she noticed, but that hadn't stopped him inviting her to sit down. What else wouldn't it stop him doing?

Once breakfast was over and Seth had cleaned up, he'd promised to take the children to the play park. Sara would ride her bike all the way, stopping at the kerb and looking back, waiting for her daddy to catch up, just as she'd been taught. Seth would tuck Olly into the baby carrier on his back. Olly loved it up there, borne along by his daddy's giant strides. He'd squeal in delight and clap his hands whenever a bus or a dog with its owner went by, and reach out to wave at the birds or to grab a branch. For Olly, everything – even the sun – was within his reach.

'I can't stay,' she said. 'I have to get back.'

He looked disappointed.

'But thank you for your help that time,' she said. 'With the bags and the oranges and everything.'

'It was nothing,' he said. 'Honestly.'

'No, really,' she replied, taking a step back. 'Thanks again.'

'You're sure I can't persuade you to stay?'

His voice was hopeful. She shook her head. 'No,' she said. 'Thank you. I really can't.'

And then she turned and left.

Olly was walking now. Proudly taking little fat steps around the back garden while Helen, in her old jeans and wellies and one of Seth's old shirts, crouched down on the ground, busily planting her rhubarb.

'You'll love it,' she'd told Seth just before she'd gone outside. 'It's so good for you. And we can freeze it and have it with porridge when winter comes round again.'

He'd pulled a face. Rhubarb. In all honesty, he wasn't keen. It was far too sharp.

'Ah, but my rhubarb is grown with love,' she'd teased. 'It'll be the sweetest rhubarb you've ever tasted.'

She'd kissed him then and hoisted Olly up onto her hip. Throwing Seth a big grin over her shoulder, off the two of them had gone. Sara was already out there, bouncing up and down on the new trampoline, limbs and hair flying in all directions.

He turned away to start on the post-lunch washing up. The kitchen floor was a disaster zone thanks to Helen's suggestion that they really ought to allow their son to feed himself. He switched on the radio and made a start. The sun was out, and despite the mess, he was happy.

Glancing out of the window, he saw Olly take a tumble, heard his cries. Immediately, Helen was on her feet, dropping her trowel and peeling off her gardening gloves. He watched her stoop to pick him up, bring his face to hers for a kiss, then swing him round. In an instant, Olly's previous mood was restored.

He caught her eye through the kitchen window and waved. She waved back, holding Olly close and pointing to the window so he could see his dad. Then she took his hand and showed him how to wave in return.

Seth didn't know where Helen had been, and he would never ask. She was back, and she loved him again. And that was enough.

First published 2017, *Woman's Weekly*

The End of the Afternoon

Even before Myra opened her eyes, she knew it had arrived. The snow. They'd been forecasting it for days. There was the light for one thing – a dazzling brightness that danced on her bedroom walls and illuminated her faded curtains.

Then there was the absence of traffic noise. On many a morning, it drowned out the clock radio alarm beside her bed, set to wake her at eight o'clock – although more often than not she'd been lying awake long before it came on. But this morning, the only sound was the shrieking of children already out playing, delighted that the weatherman's promise of a white landscape had been kept for this Saturday morning.

Once out of bed, Myra stood at the window and surveyed the road. It had been a heavy fall, and from the look of the grey, lowering sky, there would be plenty more before the day was done. From this angle, it was difficult to see where the road ended and the pavement began. The neat little hedges that divided one house from another were white; the trees were white, and the roofs, too. There was, it seemed to Myra, no other colour in the world.

She shivered and tightened the belt on her dressing gown. Well, she knew where she'd be spending the day, that was for sure. Downstairs, she made her porridge and sat at the kitchen table, staring out of the window at the vast, unsullied tundra that was her back garden.

Normally, she read the paper as she drank her morning tea. But the paperboy hadn't arrived yet. No doubt he was struggling to complete his round on foot, as it would be impossible to ride a bike today.

When her phone rang, she jumped. It was her neighbour, Annie, newly retired but still younger than her by more than ten years. She'd proved a good friend when Norman had died, bringing her food, popping round with news, inviting her for a coffee – little lifelines she'd grabbed onto gratefully, because although she couldn't eat the food or care particularly about the news or even drank coffee these days, she thought that all these things probably mattered, though she couldn't quite see it yet and would have preferred to keep the curtains shut and the doors locked. It must have paid off, though, because all these months after Norman's death, Annie still hadn't abandoned her.

'Dear me, Myra, I've never seen snow like it,' Annie said after she'd said hello. 'John can't get the car out of the drive and that's why I'm calling. I'm sending him off on foot to do some errands, so if there's anything you think you'll need for the next few days, perhaps you can give me a ring back within the next half hour.'

'That's very kind of you,' Myra said, her voice, unused as it was these days, sounding rusty in her ears

'Not at all,' Annie said. And Myra knew she meant it.

It didn't take more than a couple of minutes to make her list. She didn't want to weigh poor John down with heavy goods, since she guessed he'd be setting off against his will anyway. Bread. Cheese. A couple of packet soups. Maybe he could pop into the pharmacy to pick up her prescription, and to the newsagent's to check on the whereabouts of her newspaper. If it wasn't too much trouble.

It wasn't, John said, when half an hour later he rang the doorbell. In fact, he added, he was quite looking forward to his outing. He was bundled up in several layers, with his trousers tucked into wellies and a funny hat on his head, which he described as a beanie when Myra commented that at least his ears would be warm.

'Can't say how long I'll be,' he said, with a cheery wave. 'I may, in fact, be some time.'

Recognising the reference, Myra laughed. It was a good sound and took her through the next hour or so while she did her chores. Keeping busy kept her bleak thoughts at bay. She had some washing to do, a spot of ironing and the floors could do with a mopping.

Perhaps today was the day to think about clearing out Norman's half of the wardrobe, and his drawers, too, since she couldn't get out of the house. But not yet. Better to wait until John returned with her stuff. She wouldn't want to embarrass him by letting him catch her in any way upset.

John arrived back an hour later, his cheeks pink and his eyes bright. He looked, Myra thought, like a schoolboy who'd been given the day off. He wouldn't come in, he said, hanging over her bags in tandem with his news. She'd be happy to know the paperboy was on his way, but he'd be later than usual, and here was her prescription.

Myra was sad that he'd decided not to cross her threshold. It was her own silly fault for having mopped both the hall and kitchen floor. Of course John wouldn't want to come dribbling dirty snow all over her surfaces, such a considerate man as he was. She should have waited. Tackled the other job first. But she was rather tired now after her exertions of the morning. She'd do it after lunch.

Lunch came and went. While she waited for her soup to heat up, she stood at the kitchen window. More snow was falling now, covering the tiny dents in it that a few brave birds, venturing out of their nests, had made. She felt like she was looking out at the surface of the moon.

As she ate, she attempted the crossword. Her day was marked by little treats like this, but it was a long time till the next one; her six o'clock sherry to accompany the news.

It was perhaps a mistake to turn on the fire and settle down in her favourite armchair with the afternoon play. She fell asleep before it finished, waking suddenly, unaware of where she was. As ever, her first waking thought was of Norman. But it was no use. She couldn't resurrect him.

It took her a few moments, once on her feet, to steady herself. Ah, yes. Today. Annie had called. John had popped round to take her shopping list. 'I may be some time,' he'd joked. She smiled. Then she remembered the job she'd promised herself she'd do, and her smile faded. *I don't have to do it now,* she told herself. *I can do it tomorrow. Or the day after. Or even the day after that. But not now.*

It was far too early to draw the curtains, but what was left of the day to salvage? It was the end of the afternoon. She stood at the living room window. This morning's virgin snow had been trampled. Tyre marks churned up the road. Throughout the day, groups of children had transported snow from one place to another to build their snowmen. That brief flurry of magic that had lifted her heart for a moment upon waking had already flown off.

But the view to her back garden was different. The snow lay in drifts, untouched, perfect. Tempting. Her children were grown up now. Busy. With children of their own. One or other of them was bound to ring later tonight to see how she was faring in the upheaval British snow inevitably caused. They'd be relieved when she told them that her kind neighbours were looking out for her. She'd like to offer them more relief – she knew they worried about her these days, now that she was on her own.

When they were little how they'd squealed on those rare winter mornings when they'd woken up to a white landscape. On went the hats and the mittens and the scarves. Out came the coats. There was invariably a hunt for the wellies. And then they were off.

It was a race to see who could be the first to leave their footprint in the untrodden snow. For who could resist it? No one ever again would get the opportunity to be the first person to plant their feet upon the surface of the moon. But sinking them into the cold, thick, soft snow, before anyone else had made their mark, had to be the next best thing.

Myra remembered a pair of wellies she used to wear on camping trips with the children. It took a while to scrabble through the cupboard where the coats were kept and to trawl through the pile of abandoned footwear, but she found them in the end.

Now for a coat. She settled for Norman's old wax jacket – ideal for this kind of weather. When she dipped her hands into the pockets, she pulled out a handful of old sweet wrappers. It was too late to tell him off now, she thought, as she pulled on her gloves, wrapped a scarf round her neck and opened the back door. Oddly, the thought made her smile.

'Annie, come and have a look at this.'

John had been working in his office, aka the spare bedroom, but had grown tired. And he wanted a last look at the snow before it got dark.

'What is it, love?' Annie was on her way upstairs with a cup of tea.

'Myra. She's in the garden.'

'For goodness' sake. What's she doing out there?'

'She appears to be moonwalking,' John said.

Annie, who'd arrived in the room, handed him his cup of tea and joined him at the window.

'Good heavens!' she exclaimed.

It was true. Myra was taking great strides round the garden, placing her feet carefully as she went and using her arms to help her keep her balance, her breath steaming out.

'Do you think she's losing the plot?' she said.

They watched as she bent to pick up the snow in her hands, roll it into a tight ball and hurl it at the big pine tree. Her aim was rather good, John thought.

'No,' he said. 'Actually, I think she's got it back.'

Down below, Myra, who was beginning to work up a sweat from her exertions, happened to glance up. There were Annie and John at the window. Were they watching her? Whatever for? She waved up at them excitedly. They really didn't know what they were missing stuck inside.

Annie was opening the window and calling out to her. 'Myra! Are you OK? You must be getting cold out there.'

'No. Absolutely not. Quite the opposite,' she replied.

'Is there anything you need?' Annie said.

'No. Nothing at all,' Myra called back.

But then something popped into her head that perhaps Annie could help her with.

'I'm thinking it's time I cleared out Norman's things,' she said. 'Decide what to keep and what to part with. I've been putting it off for so long now.'

'I can imagine,' Annie cried. 'It can't be easy. Do you want me to pop round later for a bit of moral support?'

'I really would appreciate it, Annie.'

'Only if you're sure it's the right thing to do.'

'Yes. It is. I really think I'm ready to take it on now,' she said.

And then, grinning, she rolled another snowball and, with a warning for them to watch out, aimed it at their window.

First published 2013, *Woman's Weekly*

After Harriet

From some foggy lair hidden deep inside her head, a long-buried memory emerges. It's of her mother, reading. Her beautiful face is composed in concentration, long legs hitched beneath her, chin resting on one hand while, with the fingers of the other, she twirls a strand of her white-blonde hair.

Liv thinks her book is probably in Norwegian, the language she and her mother always speak when they're alone, because some of the letters differ from those she's learning at school. A diagonal stroke slices through the letter 'o', and a small bubble hovers over the letter 'a'.

A diagonal stroke cuts through Liv, too. She's half Norwegian and half English, her mother tells her. It can be confusing being cut in half. When Daddy comes home, they switch to speaking English, sometimes mid-sentence. Daddy is a professor of English. He says Norwegian is like baby talk.

When she asks her mother to tell her the name of her book, Astrid explains that it's a play, entitled *Et Dukkehjem*, which means *A Doll's House*. Liv loves dolls. Will her mother read some to her, she asks? Astrid regards her with those eyes that can be so many different shades of blue. Today, they are pale enough to be almost colourless.

It's not a children's story, darling, Astrid replies. Liv is disappointed. It's about a woman who is unhappy and who leaves her husband and children to go and live a different sort of life. Does it have a happy ending, Liv wants to know.

Astrid says she doesn't know for sure. The reader has to guess the ending. Liv has already decided that the man who wrote this play couldn't have been a very good writer. Everyone knows that a story must have a proper ending.

The memory fades. Liv finds herself back in the present. Astrid's house is situated at the top of the hill. One minute it's out of view, the next, as she rounds the final bend, she's standing before it.

It's wooden, painted sky-blue, with a slatted roof, two square windows at the top and two more at the bottom. The garden is made over to lawn and surrounded by a higgledy-piggledy wooden fence. A wooden swing is suspended between two sturdy trees. There's a flagpole but no flag. What is it with Norwegians and flagpoles? Liv briefly wonders.

* * *

It's the house that has triggered off the memory of that conversation, she realises. When Astrid fled England all those years ago, abandoning Liv to return to the country of her birth. Did she expect to find herself living in her very own doll's house? And what about the end of her story? Has it been written yet? Or will Liv write it for her?

Abandoned. Such a melodramatic word and one her mother might very well take issue with. After all, Liv gave Astrid no choice. She was the first one to walk. Right out of her mother's life, at the age of eighteen. Now, twenty years later, she's walking back in.

Where to start? Most recent first, like in a CV? Finding her mother's address proved easier than Liv could ever have imagined. In these days of the global village, everyone knows someone who knows someone else. Eventually that someone else will turn out to be the very individual who knows exactly where to find the person you're looking for. Perhaps the best place to start is at the point when life was at its most simple. Back when there was just the three of them. The perfect family. Good looking, well educated, comfortable, if not exactly well off. All living together in their doll's house.

But of course, this isn't the beginning, either. There is a time before Liv, when Mum and Dad are Chris and Astrid. Perhaps the story starts here. Cambridge. The Summer of Love. 1967. Chris, a recent graduate, is filling in time teaching English as a foreign language, postponing the dreaded decision of what to do with the rest of his life. Astrid is the beautiful Scandinavian student who walks into his classroom eager to perfect her English. They fall in love. When the summer ends, she stays on, working in bars just so she can be where he is.

He is clever. He likes Cambridge and the familiarity of college life. And he loves Astrid, too, which is just as well, because she soon becomes pregnant and the reality of the sixties, which should not be confused with the folklore, means that more often than not, this situation results in marriage. So, marriage it is, which eventually leads to Liv.

Memories of the first eight years of her life are jumbled. Uneventful. If bad things happened, Liv can't recall them. Summer holidays in Norway merge into one another. Christmases are a blur. She remembers a special doll, a birthday party with a clown. A bad fall and a broken wrist and a present for being a brave girl. She is her parents' beloved child. Then Harriet was born.

Perhaps this is the real beginning.

* * *

A woman steps outside. She is tall, still beautiful, but clearly unconcerned by anything so superficial as appearance. She raises an arm, grabs her long, white hair at the nape of her neck and ties it back with one-handed, practised efficiency. She is obviously ready for work.

Liv takes a few steps backwards, hiding herself from view behind the bend. Her heart is beating fast. It's too soon. She's not ready for this meeting. Turning on her heels, she flees.

Back at her hotel, all is chaos. There's a christening party taking place, the girl at reception informs her apologetically. The dining room is closed to other guests until this evening, but if she wants to eat, she can order from the menu and someone will bring the food to her room.

Upstairs, she takes a long shower, wraps herself in the soft, white bathrobe provided and lies down on the bed. The merriment from downstairs reaches her ears. There's laughter, applause, loud cheers. Occasionally the cry of a baby, the squeal of a toddler. Plates clatter, knives and forks scrape, glasses clink.

She should ring Sarah. Yesterday, their

conversation was brief. How are you? I'm fine. How are you? I'm good. How's your hotel? Good. How's Dad? She avoided the question she really wanted to ask her daughter. Are you eating? Simple enough. But loaded. If she rang again so soon, what more would she have to add to yesterday's store of words? She would hate it if Sarah thought she was checking up on her. Sarah probably thinks Liv's checking up on her all the time. She's right, of course.

The baguette that room service delivered is a disappointment. Baguettes and paninis have taken over the world, she concludes. Astrid would only ever make sandwiches the traditional Scandinavian way. So, of course it was inevitable as the rift between them grew that Liv began to insist on a lunchbox that contained exactly what her school friends' lunchboxes contained. Two slices of tasteless white bread filled with plastic cheese cut into four squares. She didn't enjoy them, but if eating them made her mother unhappy then it was worth it.

Why don't your sandwiches have lids? her friend Lauren asked her once on a rare visit to the house. It was just the way Norwegians made them, Liv replied. Later, as events began to spiral, she would come to think that only the sandwiches were open in her house. Everyone else had something to hide.

She must have dozed off. Coming awake, she remembers the christening taking place downstairs.

The birth of a new-born baby is a happy occasion. Liv remembers being taken onto her mother's lap and being told she was soon going to have a new sister or brother.

She quickly made up her mind it would be a girl. She knew that boys existed, but she couldn't imagine why anyone would want a baby brother. As Mummy's tummy grew bigger, Liv wondered about the baby inside. Did she peep out from beneath Mummy's clothes sometimes? When she came out, would she recognise Liv?

On the night when Mummy went off to hospital, Sue came round to stay. Sue was the cleaner, but she was more than that, Mummy said, she was a friend, too. They made a card for Mummy when the call from the hospital came to say the baby really was a girl, just as Liv had said it would be.

Congratulations on the birth of baby Harriet, the card said. Harriet was Daddy's choice. He wanted a proper, English-sounding name, he said. He hated it when strangers pronounced Liv to rhyme with give instead of grieve.

Grieve was what you did when you were sad. When Harriet was born, Mummy and Daddy seemed to be very sad indeed. Mummy didn't even say thank you for the card, even though Liv had taken it round to the neighbours on both sides of the street and asked them to sign it and put kisses.

Mummy and Daddy dragged their feet and lowered their heads into their shoulders. They whispered between themselves or stopped talking whenever she came into the room. Worse was when they stopped talking to each other altogether.

When Mummy was upstairs sleeping one day, Daddy sat Liv on his lap and explained that Harriet was a Down's syndrome baby. She might take longer to sit up and walk and talk. And it might take up more of Mummy and Daddy's time to look after her. But despite everything, she was much wanted. Liv had to be patient and helpful. He talked for a long time and used words she didn't understand. Words like chromosome and complications and cognitive ability.

Liv was used to Daddy using words she didn't understand. Mummy was used to it, too. Before she decided it wasn't funny anymore, just boring, she would turn to Liv, roll her eyes and whisper show-off, and Liv would roll her eyes back. Tired of listening to his explanation, she slipped off his lap and went in search of Harriet, who lay in her crib staring up at her mobile.

'I don't care what sort of baby you are,' she said, taking her new sister's tiny hand in her own. 'I love you, Harriet.'

And she did. She really did. Even when she hated her.

* * *

Life changed after Harriet was born. Liv spent a lot more time with Sue. Sue took her to school and collected her on days that Mummy was too tired or too busy with Harriet, and when Mummy and Daddy took Harriet to the specialist, who was like a doctor but more important and probably even cleverer than Daddy.

Before Harriet, Daddy would often work from home in the spare bedroom that he called his office. He would drink coffee and walk about the room stabbing the air with his finger while he talked for ages on the phone. But these days, he left around the same time as Liv and arrived home quite late, sometimes just as she was on her way to bed. She would crouch on the landing, peep through the wooden rails and wait for him to come up and say goodnight. Sometimes, she fell asleep waiting.

Their house was what Mummy called a typical English house. Mummy preferred Scandinavian houses. She hated carpets. They were unhygienic, she said. And the ceilings were too high and the windows too narrow. They let in none of the light but all of the draught.

A draught was a current of cold air, Daddy said. A draught began to blow through their typical English house within days of Harriet coming to live with them. It chased away the sleepy warmth that Liv had grown to relish when it was just her and Mummy, sitting on the sofa together, eating bread spread with chocolate from a jar and drinking milk, both in their pyjamas and in no particular hurry to start the day. It crept through the gaps in Mummy and Daddy's conversations. It slid beneath the living room door in the evening, accompanied by Harriet's feeble cry, just when Liv was doing her best reading for Daddy. You couldn't draw the curtains against a draught because a draught would always find another way of getting inside.

Sue said Harriet wasn't any trouble. She didn't cry a lot or wake in the night, or, when she got bigger, get into all sorts. All sorts involved things like climbing and putting your finger inside an electrical socket, Sue explained. Sue explained things much more quickly than Daddy did.

Harriet smiled a lot, loved cuddles and sweet things and didn't have tantrums. So, in that respect, Sue was right. But she didn't *do* much. Except put lines round her mother's eyes where once there had been none and give her headaches so she had to go and lie down when Liv wanted help making a dress for her doll.

She sometimes put Daddy in a bad mood, too. And she was always spoiling things. Of course, she couldn't help it, but when your birthday party is cancelled because Mummy has been with her at the hospital all night and didn't have time to get everything ready, it's difficult not to wish she had never been born.

That's what Daddy thought, too. Liv heard him say it to Mummy once. She'd woken up thirsty and crept out of bed. She sat at the top of the stairs for a long time, waiting for the right moment to call out for a drink.

Before, when there was no Harriet, she would get the drink, the tissue, the music turned down, whatever it was she wanted. But she'd get something else, too. A look, a smile, a cuddle. Something that reminded her just how much she was loved. But these days, those things were mostly absent. It was almost as if she'd been forgotten.

Mummy and Daddy were quarrelling. Or rather Daddy was quarrelling, and Mummy was crying. That's when Daddy said what he said. Liv went back to bed, forgetting all about the drink she hadn't really wanted anyway. If Daddy said he wished Harriet had never been born, did that make it OK for Liv to think the same?

* * *

If this story is about Harriet, it's also about the people around her. Liv was aware of Uncle Per from a young age. He was huge, bigger even than her father. He would scoop her up in his arms as if she were just a doll and toss her in the air so that she squealed and begged to be put down. But then as soon as she was down, she demanded to be tossed in the air again.

Uncle Per wasn't really her uncle. He was a friend of Mummy and Daddy's. He visited sporadically from wherever it was he was living at the time, bringing presents and fun.

When Uncle Per came to visit, there would be a lot of eating and drinking and talking about what Mummy called the good old days. Liv didn't think those days could have been *that* good, since the stories they told and retold always seemed to involve having no money or living off boiled potatoes in cold houses with crazy people. But she always listened politely because it was manners. The best thing about these visits was the fuss Uncle Per made of Liv. Sue said he spoiled her rotten.

On this particular afternoon, Daddy had picked her up from school. Next week was half-term, so a whole seven days of freedom beckoned. They'd walked home, kicking the autumn leaves that drifted down from the tall trees lining her street. She told Daddy she was going to make a collage, and he said what a good idea and helped her to pick the best leaves. She was happy.

When Daddy put his key in the door to let them both in, she heard a man speaking softly then Mummy's voice the same. At first, she thought it was the doctor and her heart plummeted. If Harriet was poorly again there would be no one to help her with her collage. But then she saw the suitcase and the shiny bags from the airport shop and her heart immediately lifted. She went running into the lounge as fast as she could.

'Uncle Per!'

She startled them both with her loud greeting. They were sitting close together on the settee. Harriet was in Mummy's arms and Uncle Per held her tiny hand in his own and jiggled it up and down. Harriet's mouth wobbled into a smile, and she struggled to focus her wonky eyes. Liv felt a pang of jealousy. *She* was Uncle Per's Best Girl, not Harriet.

But it was OK. As soon as Uncle Per saw Liv, he let go of Harriet's hand and was out of his chair immediately, lifting her up, swinging her round, telling her how much she'd grown. She showed him her collection of leaves and told him of her plans for half-term. He told her he'd help her because he was going to be staying for a few days.

'Isn't that brilliant, Daddy?' Liv clapped her hands delightedly.

'It certainly is,' Daddy said.

He stood before the fire, rubbing his hands together, making himself bigger than he really was. Even his voice. Liv wondered why.

* * *

The whole evening stretches out ahead of her, empty. Midsummer. Even so far south, it's light for the best part of twenty-four hours at this time of year. She finds it difficult to sleep even with the black out at her window.

The christening party is over at last. Everyone's gone home and the hotel is restored to its quiet respectability. She stands at the window and looks out onto the silent street. A life takes years to live but memory skips down the years in moments. Now, Harriet's at school. Liv is a rebellious teenager. This morning, her mother reminds her that she promised to pick up Harriet at the end of the day.

'OK, I know, I won't forget,' she says.

But when she gets to school, Lauren is waiting for her at the gate. Liv knows why but hopes she's mistaken. She isn't.

'It's today.' Lauren walks towards her, takes her arm, propels her to a quiet spot, reads the drill.

'But . . .'

'No excuses.' Lauren's grip on her arm intensifies. 'You said you'd do it, and you can't back out.'

Liv didn't get to Harriet's school on time that day. And because of that, she died.

On the outside, Liv is the kind of teenage girl other teenage girls ought to envy. Tall, willowy, good skin, long blonde hair, well-spoken and clever. In the right clothes, with the right make up and a good photographer, you might even expect to see her face looking out at you from inside the pages of a glossy magazine.

But she doesn't match on the inside, and Lauren White knows it. She knows all Liv's insecurities. How she hates being taller than some of the boys, how embarrassed she gets about her cultivated vowels and by the fact that all the teachers love her because of her straight As. She knows how she suffers when she has to give her address and name her father's profession, too. Most of all, she knows just how much Liv longs to be like everyone else.

Today is the day Liv has promised to go to the precinct with Lauren.

Shoplifting.

The word alone gives Liv a sick feeling in her guts. But if she takes this challenge and succeeds, she'll finally be accepted. It's got to be worth it, even if it means being late to pick Harriet up. Her sister will just have to wait at the school gate for her, she decides.

'How comes your mum and dad didn't send you to the posh school?'

It's important not to look suspicious, Lauren has

explained. So, they make small talk as they riffle through the racks, deciding what to steal.

Liv isn't comfortable talking about her family. Her dad doesn't agree with private education, she explains. Her mum thinks everyone should go to the local school, like in Norway. Because of her condition, Harriet has to go to a school a bit further away, but it's still close enough to home for Mum to pick her up every day. Only today, she's got something on. Typical of her to get in the way of Liv's plans, she grumbles.

Lauren's not really listening. She's picked out a top. Cropped. Glittery. She holds it out to Liv. Liv thinks it looks cheap. She prefers clothes that you can blend into.

'Go and ask that snooty assistant if they've got this in a ten,' she says.

'Isn't there a ten there?' She was certain she'd just seen one in that size.

Lauren sticks her tongue in her cheek and makes her eyes meet in the middle. Liv wishes she hadn't told her about Harriet. She wants to say Harriet's face doesn't look anything like the one you're pulling.

'Tell her you've looked and looked and there isn't one. Ask her to check in the back.' Lauren presses the glittery crop top into Liv's stomach. 'Go on,' she adds. 'She'll do it for you.'

The sales assistant glances up from her nails for long enough to listen to Liv's request. She asks the same question Liv asked Lauren. No, Liv replies. We've looked and looked but there is no ten. Suspicion flickers in the assistant's eyes when she glances over at Lauren in her hoodie and jeans. She's reluctant to do Liv's bidding. But Liv smiles and the sales assistant relents.

She only turns her back for a brief second. That's all it takes. Glancing in Lauren's direction, Liv sees her roll the top into a ball and shove it up the front of her hoodie.

'Come on,' she mouths.

Liv is rooted to the spot. The assistant is strolling over to the back of the shop. If she doesn't move now, all will be lost. Lauren's already at the door.

'Hey!'

The salesgirl's seen her. Liv's reaction to her cry is panic fuelled. She takes sudden flight. Lauren's outside now, running. She's quick, but Liv's legs are longer and soon Liv's caught her up and they're side by side, laughing, dodging the startled shoppers, sending some kid flying, hearts pumping, their breath coming out in bursts. Finally, they're out of the precinct.

'That was great,' Lauren says when she's recovered her breath.

There's a light in her eyes that Liv has never seen before. Now that she's stopped running, all Liv feels is disgust and shame and an urge to get as far away as possible. She did all that just to get in Lauren's good books. But Lauren just ran off and would have left her to take the consequences. Is that what friends do?

'I've got to go and pick up my sister,' she says.

'See you tomorrow, then.'

Liv never speaks to Lauren again.

She has replayed what happens next so many times. During the year when she couldn't go to school, when she barely left her bed, let alone her room, she relived it every waking morning and last thing every night. Because she wasn't there the moment it happened, she wrote her own terrible version. In her dreams, she sometimes changed the ending. Harriet, waiting patiently outside the school gate for Liv to come and pick her up, just as Mummy had told her to do. Smiling at her as she approaches, running towards her with outstretched arms.

She must have got bored waiting and wandered off. The school was absolved of all blame. The inquest was most particular about that. It takes just a second for a child to slip a teacher's grasp and run out into the road. But the consequences last forever.

Liv's phone rings. Sarah's name flashes up. Liv's heart skips a beat.

'Darling, are you all right?' She recognises the same anxiety that once saturated her mother's voice now seep into her own. It's always a struggle to keep it at bay – she must try harder, that's all.

'Hey, Mum! Well?'

Sarah knows why Liv is here. She applauds her visit. She knows nothing about the time she prayed and the vow she made.

Whatever happens, if Sarah lives or dies, I'm going to find my mother and make things right between us.

Everyone knows you can't go back on a vow.

'Tomorrow,' she says. 'I'll visit her tomorrow. I promise.'

'Good. Hey, Dad made pizza and I ate all of it.'

'That's brilliant,' Liv says.

'Well, half of it.'

'Oh. That's still good.'

'Because there was chocolate mousse for afters, and I had to save a space for that.'

Liv laughs. 'Even better,' she says.

They chat some more. It's comfortable between them. Sarah's having some friends round. They've been arguing about which DVD to watch. In fact, she needs to get back on MySpace to make sure they haven't ganged up on her while she's been on the phone and decided on the film she doesn't want to see.

'Tomorrow, remember,' Sarah says, before she says goodbye.

'Tomorrow,' Liv promises.

And now tomorrow is today. Another blue sky, the sun big and bright. The little Scandinavian town is like something out of a fairy tale. There should be a palace and horse-driven carriages, Liv thinks. Instead, a town hall with pink walls and bright shiny trams criss-crossing the streets will have to suffice.

Liv called home again this morning, after breakfast. Jack is upbeat. Sarah is definitely on the mend, he says. Her eyes are shining, and her skin is clear. She's full of energy. And she's eating. So, her prayers have been answered. She has no excuses left.

Sarah was anorexic. Liv's illness didn't have a name, just a list of symptoms that had no end. Both lost a whole year of their lives at the age of seventeen.

Sarah's symptoms crept up on her, whereas Liv was struck down on the very same night Harriet died. No one said they blamed her. Not her father nor her mother. It was just unfortunate that Harriet chose to slip away when Liv was in charge, they both insisted. It could equally have happened had either of them been a little late to pick Harriet up.

But it didn't. It happened on her watch, so the guilt was all hers. She took to her room. That way, she could avoid having to witness her family falling apart around her.

She remembered little of the months that followed. Her mother's bleak face, her father's woeful

147

attempts at normality. The stifling atmosphere of loss and mourning. Such was the breadth of her insularity that she spectacularly failed to notice her mother's pregnancy.

Harriet died in the September. The following September, when her new brother was three months old and when all her friends were going off to other parts of the country to begin new lives at different universities, Liv went back to school.

Her father, shelving his principles about private education, paid for her to attend a very expensive crammer, where she could quickly be brought up to speed in all her subjects, ready for A levels the following year.

Liv discovered she quite liked it there. There were no gangs, no populars, no jocks – just a bunch of individuals who, like herself, had gone through stuff they really didn't want to talk about and were fortunate to have parents who had the means to give them a second chance. She kept her head down, made progress and began to see a point to life again.

But though school helped, it was Oskar's magic that transformed their family, albeit briefly. He immediately became the family's focal point. Liv adored him. Plucking him from his baby bouncer, holding him close and taking in his sweet, warm smell restored her.

He was all those things Harriet had been – smiley, amenable, loving – and many things she hadn't been, too. He walked at ten months, and once he got his first words, others tumbled from his sweet lips in one long, cheerful monologue.

And because of Oskar, the elephant in the room that had taken up residence the day Harriet died lay down in the corner and made itself, if not invisible, then as small as any elephant could manage. It didn't stay there for long, however.

Liv applied to university. She got offers. She began to look forward to her new life. She met a nice boy in her class and they briefly dated. But she wasn't ready for romance.

She decided she preferred books and wondered if she was doomed to turn into her father, which was not at all what she aspired to do. Academics dissected everything. They couldn't just be happy in the moment. If she had a choice, she'd rather be like Uncle Per, still dipping in and out of their lives bringing presents. Though now he'd swapped the dolls for perfume and chocolates.

One week before her exam results were due out, Uncle Per visited. He was passing through on his way back to Norway, where he'd taken a new job. Her father teased him about how quickly he'd turn into a typical Norwegian once back in his homeland. Would he have his own log cabin, just like his father's, where he could go fishing in the summer and skiing in the winter?

Dad hated anything to do with the outdoors. He

liked to talk. And Norwegians weren't big on talking, he said. They sat in the living room and played with Oskar while Dad alternately made feeble Norwegian jokes and boasted about his new book. Astrid rolled her eyes at Liv, who rolled hers back. As long as Oskar was around, they were united.

Oskar shrieked with delight, scrunching his little fists so they dimpled up like rising dough. Per couldn't get enough of looking at him. How like Oskar he was, Liv thought. Both blonde and big and uncomplicated.

Even a bubble popped will leave a trace, a memory of itself in the air, and now it was impossible to put back the thought. In that moment, Liv became certain that Oskar was Per's son.

* * *

Something is happening at Astrid's house. A party is being prepared. All the doors have been flung open; there's music, and a ladder is propped up against a wall. It's been a long climb in the heat of the day. Liv stops to draw breath. Shielding her eyes against the sun, she trains her gaze on the figure at the top of the ladder. He appears to be fixing bunting and swearing as it steadfastly refuses to go where he wants it to go.

At first, she thinks it must be Per. But Uncle Per would be sixty or more, and this is a young man. And then she realises it must be Oskar. She takes a few steps forward to confirm her suspicions. Dizziness strikes her and she stumbles, grabbing hold of the fence to stop herself from falling. By the time she recovers, he is by her side, taking her arm and helping her into the garden, where he insists she must sit down and rest.

He'll fetch her a glass of water, he says, addressing her in Norwegian. He'd call his mother – she's a nurse, something else new for Liv to take in – but his parents have gone into town to pick up a cake. Then he dashes inside.

How could she have forgotten? Oskar's birthday falls on June 21st. Midsummer's Eve. Oskar is a young man now. He has his mother's eyes, she realises. Her half-brother and the cause of that terrible argument with her parents that led to the break-up of her family and the long separation that she now hopes to bring to an end.

The memory of what happened when Liv realised Oskar was Uncle Per's son unfolds as if it were yesterday. She remembers the cruel pleasure she got from plotting just how and when she would confront her mother and throw her secret right back in her face.

In the event, it was her father she confronted first. To this day, she has no idea why. They'd had a difference of opinion, probably over some book or other. Her father only ever discussed literature with her. The discussion of anything more personal made him nervous.

Oskar was asleep upstairs. Astrid was out. They were in the kitchen. A bottle of wine stood half empty on the table. It wasn't his first of the evening. Her father was drinking far too much these days. Liv decided to tell him so. It clouds your judgement, she added, feeling smug.

'What do *you* know?' he said, his tone bitter, his expression scathing.

So, she told him. 'I know that Oskar's not your son.'

What a fool she must have been to utter those words. How naïve to imagine herself to be the only person who knew the truth. As if her father had no eyes and no intelligence. She'd humiliated him, and now he would have to return the favour.

'So, you think you're better informed than I am, do you?' he said.

She had no idea what he meant and said so. In that case, perhaps he'd better fill her in, he said, slurring his words. Astrid was with Per. Astrid was always with Per. If not in body, then in spirit. In fact, he added, curling his lip as if it gave him pleasure to inflict this final blow, Astrid was with Per on the very afternoon that Harriet was run over. Coincidentally, the very afternoon that little Oskar, upstairs fast asleep right now, was conceived.

Liv remembers little of what happened next. A moment of numb shock and then, as the pieces of the jigsaw slotted into place, the certainty that her father spoke the truth. She felt the pulse of blind fury in her veins. It was just as it reached boiling point that her mother chose to turn the key and let herself in.

Had she really attacked Astrid? Yes. She remembers the startled look in her mother's eyes as she touched her cheek and saw blood on her fingers. She remembers screaming and ranting a torrent of accusations.

Her mother had used her to run an errand while she'd been spending the afternoon in bed with Per. It was *her* job to pick up Harriet – not Liv's. It wasn't *her* fault that Harriet had died; it was her mother's.

She remembers her mother screaming back, do you think I don't know that? Over and over, falling to the ground, sobbing loud tears, saying that she would never forgive herself for Harriet's death. But her tears failed to move Liv. By now, fury had burned itself out, to be replaced by cruel indifference. She was as cold as marble.

'I never want to speak to you again,' she said, storming out of the room and leaving her parents to mend the broken pieces she'd left behind. As if they ever could.

How self-righteous she'd been. A young girl with no experience of life or love, making the mistake of believing herself to be the only one who hurt. Ten years later, at her father's funeral, she learned why her mother had turned to Per for love. Dad's new wife, her tongue loosened with alcohol, admitted that their affair had started not long after Harriet was born. Just at a time when Astrid needed a husband's support most. Was it surprising she turned to her old friend, her countryman, for the support her husband couldn't provide?

The day after Liv's outburst, Astrid left with Oskar. Liv didn't know where they'd gone and cared even less. In her wilful fury, she even hated Oskar. As if a child could be to blame for what had occurred. Moodily, she hung around the house until it was time to go to university. She meant what she said and broke all ties with her mother. She and her father rubbed along without resolving anything.

When she came back home for Christmas, he announced that he and Astrid were getting a divorce. On returning for the summer holidays, she found he'd moved a girlfriend in. When it became apparent that the girlfriend was a permanent fixture, Liv decided she wouldn't bother coming home again during the holidays. She had her own friends now. They would be her family.

* * *

'Your water.'

'Thanks.'

The sound of an engine groaning up the hill causes them both to turn their heads.

'Mum and Dad,' he says, grinning ruefully. 'I keep telling them to get that old car fixed.'

She realises that any second now, Liv and Per will be driving into the yard and getting out of their car. She spills the water. It's all happening too quickly. She isn't ready. She can't do it.

If Sarah doesn't survive, you will have to live with your grief for the rest of your life.

This was the thought that had run around in her head during those dark months when her daughter was in and out of hospital battling her illness.

She thought of her own mother, imagining how she must have suffered as she waited at the hospital to hear if Harriet had survived the accident. And then the despair when it became apparent she hadn't. Mixed with this the guilt.

If only I, I never should have . . .

This was the conclusion she arrived at. The tragedy of a daughter's death was a thing they could share. But not if they never saw each other again. They would be like two of those little fishing boats Liv glimpses on the horizon when she takes her walk down to the seafront each morning after breakfast. Each marooned out on the big wild ocean, far from the shore, alone and lost.

And if the best thing happened and Liv's prayers were answered, and Sarah survived, then her survival should be celebrated. She had a grandmother, an uncle, maybe cousins, none of whom she knew. It was time to remedy that situation.

The car doors slam. People are getting out. A man. A woman. Joking, laughing, struggling with the cake. Careful your end. Watch that corner.

Liv can't bear to look up and take that first glimpse of her mother's face. But she needs to – that's why she's here.

As the car pulled up, Oskar had jumped up and left her side to hurry over and help rescue his precious cargo. He is speaking now, explaining why there is a stranger in their garden drinking a glass of water. She feels eyes on her, the voices still, the mood change.

And then she hears a mighty crash, followed by footsteps on the grass. And suddenly, standing before her, is Astrid.

Momentous occasions such as these demand momentous words. Later that night, as she sits round the Midsummer bonfire with Astrid on one side and Per on the other, drinking aquavit with them and talking through the years, oblivious to the party going on around them, she decides their own first exchange would never stand up to the scrutiny of scholars. What was it she'd said now? Something about the cake, that's right.

'Oh, dear! You've dropped Oskar's birthday cake! It must be ruined.'

She'd spoken in English and then repeated the words in Norwegian. For good measure, she'd added one more banality. 'Let me help you pick up the pieces. Perhaps it can be fixed,' she'd said.

Then Astrid had given her reply. 'We'll fix it together, shall we?'

First published 2012, *Fiction Feast*

Something Different

It was Monday. A grey, damp Monday. Evie lay in bed, eyes closed, listening to the rain slide down her windowpane. In her head, she played out the routine before her. Feed cat, have breakfast, take shower, get dressed, put on face, head for bus stop. In all, it would take seventy-nine minutes. She'd timed it. Craig once said she had OCD.

She would enjoy it for a minute more, just lying here and being lazy. It puzzled her how contented she felt, considering it was only the start of the week and not the end. Considering it was raining. Considering that before her lay eight hours of telephone marketing, a job she'd never really thought she was cut out for. Sometimes, when she got home after a day smiling and being pleasant on the phone, her jaw ached with the effort of it all.

'What's up with you?' Craig would say. 'It's a job, isn't it?'

She sniffed the air. It smelled different. When she was a child, special days smelled like this. Birthdays. Christmas. The first day of the school holidays. It was the smell of promise, and this morning it beckoned her from her bed.

As a rule, she never sang. Not even when she was alone. She had a horrible voice, Craig said. There was contempt in the cat's eyes as – warbling away – she spooned out his breakfast.

'I'm good, aren't I?' she said, staring him out.

He raised his right paw and licked it. He did this every morning, pretended to have something more important to do than eat his breakfast. Just to show her who was boss.

'You old silly,' she said. 'You're only a cat, you know.'

But to show there were no hard feelings, she gave him an extra dollop of Yummy Paws and tickled him under the chin.

She sang in the shower, too, this morning. And while she dressed and put on her make up, she found herself making a special effort. It may be raining and a Monday, but the world was out there, and it was full of possibilities.

Outside, there were clouds, damp, drizzle. But beyond them, if you looked with your other senses, you could glimpse sweet air, touch all the colours of a rainbow, taste sunlight. The pot-holed streets were golden pavements.

Some mornings she had to stand on the bus. She never minded. She was a door; shut, locked and bolted. This morning, though, she felt herself swing open, and the world came rushing in. If the bus conductor had ever smiled at her before, she'd never noticed, at least not for a while. When he smiled this morning, she smiled back.

A boy in school uniform offered her his seat. She thanked him, told him how kind it was of him. The old gentleman next to her said it was a turn-up, someone giving up their seat like that, especially a kid, and it just went to show how there was a lot of nonsense spoken about the younger generation.

She didn't turn her head away like she would have done yesterday. She said, 'Yes!' and 'Absolutely!' and 'How right you are!' And for the rest of the journey, she felt the connection between them like an invisible thread.

'You look different this morning,' said her co-worker, Jane, as she threw her coat over her chair and took her seat beside her. 'What have you had done?'

'Have you changed your hair or something?' Melanie said at lunchtime, as they waited in the canteen queue. 'There's something different about you today.'

'Are you wearing a new foundation?' Cathy asked,

as Evie grabbed a break by the water cooler. 'You're looking as fresh as a daisy.'

No, she said. And no. And no again. They must just be imagining things.

She called at the expensive deli en route home. Today was a day to celebrate and spoil herself. She chose a full-flavoured brie, some smoked olives, a jar of roasted peppers, one hundred grams of bresaola, wafer-thin. Girly food, Craig called it. Craig was a meat and two veg man. She asked if she could have just half a loaf.

'Dining alone this evening?' Mario, the shop owner, asked her, as he expertly obliged, slicing the loaf in two with his fancy machine.

'No,' she said. 'Tonight, I have company.'

'Then you'll need wine,' he said. 'No party is complete without it.'

'Certo,' she replied. 'Absolutely.'

They left on good terms. She hadn't spent much, but she had made a stab at his beautiful language. From now on, they were friends.

Then she was home. She took off her coat, kicked off her shoes and put her food away. She cuddled the cat and fed him, keeping him company while he ate. Later, their positions would be reversed.

'Dining alone this evening?' Mario had asked. Oh, no. Tonight she would be dining with a very dear friend. They'd lost touch recently. It happened like that sometimes, when a man came along.

161

The man had moved out a month ago. Oh, how she'd cried. How she'd missed him, lost sleep over him, read his old emails and his texts over and over, as if she could reclaim him through his words.

But then this morning. Sniffing the air. Sensing the promise. She was over him. He was gone. When she thought of him it was only briefly. A thing he did, a habit he had. No, he hadn't been the one for her. She deserved much better from a man.

Her face in the mirror gleamed with some of that spirit she hadn't seen in a long while. She was back. The one who knew her best. Who cared for her the most.

'I've missed you. We have a lot of catching up to do,' she said to her reflection. 'So, care to have dinner with me tonight?'

First published 2017, *Woman's Weekly*

About the Author

Geraldine Ryan is a proud Northerner who has spent most of her life in Cambridge – the one with the punts. She holds a degree in Scandinavian Studies, but these days only puts it to use when identifying which language is being spoken among the characters of whatever Scandi drama is currently showing on TV. For many years, she worked as a teacher of English and of English as a second or foreign language, in combination with rearing her four children, all of whom are now grown-up, responsible citizens. Her first published story appeared in *My Weekly* in 1993. Since then, her stories have appeared in *Take a Break, Fiction Feast* and *Woman's Weekly,* as well as in women's magazines abroad. She has also written two young adult novels – *Model Behaviour* (published by Scholastic) and *The Lies and Loves of Finn* (Channel 4 Books.) She plans for *Riding Pillion with George Clooney* to be the first of several short story anthologies.

Keep up to date with Geraldine's news, be the first to hear about her new releases and read exclusive content by signing up to her monthly newsletter *Turning the Page*. By adding your details, you'll also receive a free short story. Use this link to subscribe: https://bit.ly/Turningthepage

 twitter.com/GeraldineRyan

Printed in Great Britain
by Amazon

·

18564534R00099